Alex Kujawa lives in Totland Bay, Isle of Wight, writes stories in his free time…also does judo, speaks French, loves films of all genere and reads a lot of books in his spare time which inspired him to do creative stories.

I would like to thank the team at my work place, Inglefield Nursing Home, Totland Bay, Isle of Wight, for the inspiration and giving me the characters in the story that helped me write this novel.

Alex Kujawa

MAD MYSTERY

AUSTIN MACAULEY PUBLISHERS™
LONDON • CAMBRIDGE • NEW YORK • SHARJAH

A CIP catalogue record for this title is available from the British Library.

ISBN 9781398471191 (Paperback)
ISBN 9781398473423 (ePub e-book)

www.austinmacauley.com

First Published 2024
Austin Macauley Publishers Ltd®
1 Canada Square
Canary Wharf
London
E14 5AA

Mark, Kiera, and the others enter the Care Home in 2023. An accident happens. They don't know someone called Julie Kid Long is seeking revenge because of this. The rest do not trust other humans and live in isolation.

Thirteen years later, in 2036, at the same home the night before Halloween, Hannah and her group of friends go inside. As the barrier closes, they realise they are trapped. The lighting strikes the home during the daytime and it gives her friends kind of superpowers. Time is against them. They have clues around the home which is spinning, flipping, and turning upside-down, and also has a ghost roaming around.

It is time the ghost lets go of the past and puts their trust in Hannah and her friends to save the day before history repeats itself. Now they need the ghost's help to stop Julie Kid Long. Together, they are strong but the question is can the ghost trust these humans home after what happened all those years ago and what they had been through.

Can Hannah and the ghost join forces and end the reign of Julie Kid Long before the Halloween Party starts…

Prologue

On October 30, the day before Halloween, in 2023, the wind is blowing hard and leaves are falling out of the trees. The building is called Taunting Home. This one in particular is bizarre; things are out of place, creaking noises are heard, curses and ghosts; especially ghosts.

A young girl walks into the building—a chirpy smile and polite. She walks in as I get dressed for work. I spot Mark following Kiera as she passes with a trolley of hot drinks and juices as he was shadowing her. Sherry comes moments behind, gears up, and walks into the room. Kiera puts on an apron and gloves. She delivers the drinks as we go back to the tea room.

I am about to go up the stairs when the cleaner, Lolly, comes down the stairs two at a time in a rush for something. She says hi to us and all of us reply back. As she answers the door, there is nothing there…

Just an envelope…

Seconds later, Charlette comes down as Lolly is still holding the paper. Lolly gets the affirmative from her and opens it and begins to read: "People of Taunting the home, it is locked until Halloween Night, 31 October. Let the puzzle begin…"

While listening to the news, a whoosh of cold air pierces the home. I shiver as it made my spine tingle. Then something breaks and pieces of glass shatter everywhere. I approach it. I feel a hand stretch and grab my shirt then. My skin turns ice cold as I push away this hand.

It has a strong grip but I break the grip yet it's still holding my wrist. My heart turns at a rapid rate and my breathing stops. Mark runs and slides on his knees towards me and I fall into his arms. His hands instantly change from pink to purple-blue because of no circulation and I watch him save me as the home blurs.

I wake up in a bedroom and look around. Coming to my senses, I look up at the ceiling. There is a mirror and it showed my reflection with all cracks. I hop out the bed and stumble towards the door and find the handle. It was the corridor. Floating along, I find that the rest are okay. Out of nowhere another ghost appears.

It was Mark and Kiera, and also Sherry; either one wouldn't speak. I head to the stairs to go down to the floor below and watch the rest move. I see Lolly, Richard, Tillie, two more cleaners, and Hannah doing drinks on the Middle Floor. I feel I'm missing out but then a voice says, "We are dead, living in the afterlife. We live in the same building one day later."

My mind is processing the words as everything spins like a spinning top. I see the blackboard and in chalk, the date written is 31 October 2023. The bell alarm system rings and it reads Room 44. I shuffle along down the corridor and something flies past me so fast, I move and hit the wall. I whisper, "I am a ghost but can feel things in this place."

I scan my hands which are perfectly fine but my feet don't touch the floor; I gasp. A voice says, "Go there, hold positions." I come round the corner and see all carers that were in the accident—Stan, Mia, Sherry, Mark, myself, and Charlette. Also, there is someone else. As Charlette holds a device, the radios haywire and light bulbs break.

We see a dark ink on the wall stretching and it grabs for the group but they dodge. It continues to move and a bright white light flashes, blinding us. The last thing is Charlette sings, "Things will be safe and it will not come back." The doors slam shut and I hear the click of a key turning. This person says they will get revenge.

Chapter 1
Hoping the Humans Do Not Open This Door

Taunting Home. Thirteen years later, the year is 2036. I start somewhere new as I pass a barrier. Just on the other side is the car park. Walking up, I see bins on the right and flowers in the middle leading to the main entrance. Seconds later, one person comes in. He is tall, bulky, strong, funny at times, and chatty. Walking next to him is Lolly.

I wait as it reopens and two more come through the barrier. The first one is of normal height, has blond hair, a T-shirt, a skirt, and green eyes. The other has brownish hair, a T-shirt, long trousers, blue eyes, and glasses. About to reach the door when the barrier splits open again. The last person comes through with a medium height, smart, always punctual, and kind; this one had a nice attitude.

The barrier explodes a purple light, shooting to the sky, indicating that this will not open again. Then something shakes all way down and passes the people who waltz through. We all look at the sun shining bright as we start working on one thing. My mother tells me that it is important not to go into Room 44.

In the tea room, I prepare the trolley for the round. The machine constantly produces hot water in a small space. Through the hatch to the kitchen, the radio is playing rock and roll music. "Mystery come in and have fun join." I crouch to get something under the sink and a voice goes, 'Boo!' I hit the sink (really painful just so you know).

I saw nothing so I continue. Voices bounce in the room making me feel someone is here with me in this very room; impossible. I breathe and shake my head. I place the cups on the trolley but it slides to the bac. I grab it, move a little to the right and release my hand. The cup reverts to its original position. Look through the trolley it's the door to the lift. Still nothing heard.

I hear a rattling noise which brings me back to reality. It was Paige with her medical trolley. She smiles and reads off the phone what she needs then disappears into the room. I step out into the corridor. The machine blows and pieces fly and I turn away. As I turned, I see the cups moving.

Sugar, tea bags, and hot water in the white jugs, and milk from the fridge is placed on the trolley. I rub my eyes and see Paige. I go towards her and she looks at me. Something moves on her trolley.

Paige and I see this. The needle rises along with the bottle in the box which is placed on top. It joins the needle and pulls back with the right measurement surprisingly. She points and I follow her finger to see my trolley move. As the door closed, the trolley rolls towards me and I sidestep out of the way. Paige joins me as both trolleys move.

Mine goes straight on Paige's medical trolley past us towards the kitchen. I follow mine and she walks to hers. The trolley stopped right at the entrance. A cup flies right in my face and I raise both hands and grab the thing; it said Room 13. Once there, I walk in and place it down. The response was thankyou but there is nobody in the room.

Past the dining place, I grab the trolley and push it myself till the other end. The trolley turns for the lift and as I go to turn towards the rooms, the doors open…

A ghost pushes into the lift as it slipped from my fingers. I go after it but standing in the lift, she huffs. Her reflection waves to me but there's nothing in front of me. I press button 1 for the Middle Floor. In the mirror, there is my reflection and this one on the right, and as I stare, she squeezes and blood splats all over the mirror.

Nausea in my stomach builds and I'm about to vomit. As the doors open, I push the trolley fast out of the lift allowing myself to breathe. A voice laughs and the lift descends into emptiness. The ghost in the lift is still here but she pushes the trolley. I follow behind her all the way to the end of the corridor.

She says that we'll meet again and then nothing. I'm all alone. Right, continue. As I reach the lift, the door opposite opens and a hand is thrust right out behind me. I turn to see and its bone structure snaps while turning. I continue towards the rooms at the end. When done, I make a right turn down this long corridor heading to the Wing.

I push the trolley and as I step, my feet splash something but it was just the carpet, and it was like this until the end. I get there and see Paige. I had all floors to do and next is the Middle Floor after the Wing. I'm happy to see her. It's still a mystery why are jobs done while we're here.

The board behind me wrote a message 'You have until 21:00pm tonight or both homes are destroyed.' As the chalk rubs away, Paige and I look at each other making no sense at all. We wait as Dixie comes round the corner to clean the rails and goes straight to Middle Floor. The building shakes.

I go to the corridor and the view moves clockwise and the ground goes to the top; Middle Floor turns left and drops; the left is shifted to the bottom as I watch. The Top Floor is now up this long corridor. Dixie says, "The Middle is now ground," and laughs.

I go straight and get in the lift, go to the ground, and make drinks. In the Wing, I tell myself to ignore Room 44, come back, and go towards the lift. I step inside and the floor is made of glass, and the whole thing shifts.

Chapter 2
The World Turns Upside-Down

I stood still to see the buttons. I spot one underneath the one which has a zero on it and press that. As the door close, on the glass floor a hand slams hard. I slide as I face Hannah. "Hello, Hannah! Come play a puzzle." It fists the glass as it begins to move. The door opens and I find myself at the car-park. All blue and white as clouds in the sky.

The door closes again and there's a bang on the metal. The rail behind me rips off the wall and another door appears, I find myself back in the home and as the rail swings, I dive to the floor. It scratches the carpet. I see Dixie with her cleaning trolley spraying a chemical. She looks at me and asks me if I was fine.

I stand up nodding to her and she prods along the corridor cleaning away. She smiles and I feel something inside, like a friendship building. The carpet changes colour which I decided to ignore. I head to the stairs. Walking up, feeling in the building the resonation of the steps…I make it to the landing.

A loud crunching sound is heard and I turn. I find the stairs moving. The bottom ones rose and pierced the wall. I attach the others heading up as the wooden handles in the middle fell and I make steps flipping, clockwise steps, heading to the first floor. I spin around and walk past the office. There is another door on the right and this one needs to be pushed harder than before.

It flings open and there are shelves of things—a mix tape, auto-rewind 80s cassette. A tape slides on the floor and I take hold of it. A white light shines, breaking it apart. I watch as it smashes into pieces and something shoots like a bullet heading for me. I close my eyes and it vanishes before it reaches me. I hear the words "Will get revenge." I look at this tape.

I march to view the office and see that the desk is empty. There is a machine that looks the right size for the tape. I step quietly, one at a time. Once close enough, I stretch for the machine. I stop in my tracks as I hear voices. It was hard to not move.

I try to reach it with my fingertips and feel with my hand the machine sliding across the hard floor. As the voices still chat, I listen while focusing on the task at hand. I finally have this thing and it is time to find what this mix tape can do. I head to the Activity Arena.

I get there, breathing hard. There is nothing in the room. The machine had a headphone hole and the wire is there. I place these Sony Walkman headphones and the room changes. People are happy, singing, and doing stuff for Halloween Party which is tonight. I walk further into the room as there is something in the window. It was a ghost smiling, which terrifies me.

The ghost starts moving from the windows. At the end of the table, it jumps to the right and I follow the windows. While walking forwards, he bumps. The expression on his face is angry as he rubs his nose and shakes his head. He breathes and says, "Sorry, my manners are atrocious. Let's start with introductions. My name is…"

I turn round with the headphones to see the ghost who was pushing my trolley all day and the one who did Paige's medicines all coming to help. "Get lost," she said.

The ghost in the window laughs and began to speak in an upset tone, "Sorry to hear that." They all stare at her and she changes to a laughing tone.

"Hannah, it will happen before you know it," and sticks her tongue out, jumps up, and spins in a circle, shaking her body, she jumps up and down. She flicks her hand and the radio plays music. I shove off the headphones and the room is back to normal. I can't see but hear them. It was my chance. I was about to put on the headphones but lighting strikes the floor in front of me. There's no hole, no damage done. White light fires at me into the home.

The ghost talked and they said these words, "Halloween night, I will rule the Care Home and there are clues everywhere also objects to help the ceremony." It came from the one locked in the room I am not allowed to open. I stumble backwards out into the home and run to the Middle Floor. I stop to see a room, it was 23, the one opposite the lift. I watch the window and there is light.

As I step forward, the black ink on the door handle forms a hand and grips my hand. I yell but it pulls me into the room. The door stays open so I take in the atmosphere. I whack the hand and it lets me go and retracts back to the bed. I place my feet and feel something squishy. I peer down and it was an eye. It explodes and I get covered in blood.

I wipe my eyes to see the bed and approach the edge and touch the rail. My foot touches something and my eyes peer down. I crouch to see vines; it whisks under the bed and I watch in anticipation. I stand up slowly. The black ink on the rail attacks me but I move out of the way. It smashes photos into the wall and I fall backwards out into the hallway. The ink changes form into a key laying on the floor.

I place the headphones on. I sing along to the song playing *Piece of the puzzle*. The drums and guitar intro of twenty seconds in the song begins. The key wriggles and jumps vigorously as I start the next words, "Let's play a game in the home." The key splits apart and I figure this destroys it. The next words are, "Find the missing piece. A piece of a puzzle," said really loud, and then the ink key was gone.

I get up and sort my clothes out which are covered in blood. As I see Richard, the song continues. As I sing, more things were appearing in front of me. An X-ray of his body indicates his body structure is changeable and flexible – statues and stones, books, watches allow to do things but glasses and people with nightmare curse. Then something came in front of me.

It is a blue light. A person. It is a woman; tall, with long legs and arms, brown hair, and 6 feet. It is Sherry, the carer. I gasp!

Chapter 3

On the machine, I press the pause button. She sees me and I wave to her. She shakes her head and I wait for her to speak. It didn't matter and left in a hurry. I place the cassette of the 80s mix player away as Richard talks to me, saying his body is doing things and he had gloves on points to the wooden rail. My eyes follow and make sure I was touching nothing. I search for Tillie and Paige and find both in the tea room.

I watch as Tillie says what happened and listen. As Paige pours hot water from the machine, a splash lands on her arm but she doesn't even flinch, not even an 'ow that hurts'. I did a headcount of people who were here—Paige, Richard, Tillie, Hannah, Lolly, and Dixie, but where was Dixie? She is right here at the door cleaning nothing. She smiles and her skin camouflages before my eyes.

We are all here and it makes no sense. I remember the lighting striking everyone but Tillie and me, and now all of them have powers. As I place the headphones on, I see Sherry passing me, Stan – the kitchen porter and Mia with her red hair, lipstick, and round body stood in fear. Then a person comes out waking up. He is tall, skinny, with blond hair, blue eyes, and laughingly thanks us.

At 09:00am, the building shakes. I tell them about the incident in the Activity Arena. "I have something that allows me to see things you can't at the moment." We all decide to work together. The lift doors open and a ghost stands there right in the middle of the room. It lifts its hands and a ball of ink makes a key turn.

The lock on the mirror clicks and pushes it open. It steps onto the floor of the home and whistles. A trolley moves towards it and we move out of the way it made. It throws the trolley, closes the door, and was gone for good before it says to us, "Do you like Puzzle, Hannah? Oh well, too late. The puzzle has begun starting with the Activity Arena Room and party on Halloween Night. Everything you love is gone." It smiles as the doors close.

I did the jugs of squash before another round of teas. Paige went to fetch her cabinet of medication and goes round. The rest went back to laundry and cleaning the rooms. I went to put the jugs but I remembered there is no trolley because the ghost locked it away for good in the lift. So, no more teas. On the fridge lay a tray to carry the jugs in multiple stages instead…

…Blood on the floor reaches ankle deep. The sink burst with waste, covering me from head to toe. Then an eye hits me in the face. I find myself sitting in the pool of blood. Another eye comes flying. As I try moving backwards, my feet get stuck. I lift them up and down my leg, there is a tangle of tenders and joint muscles.

The shelf on the right has hands that had no fingers, with blood pouring out, blue purple as the circulation is cut-off, and an urn made of bones. In the kitchen, the sink is bubbling and a hand pops through the surface. It's all black and it grabs the metal sink, pulling more like it's never-ending. The radio plays loud music.

I manage to move again and fall out of the room. It reverts suddenly and I find the tray filling the jugs for ground going to each room. I get the device out, put the headphones in, and listen to the song. It goes like this, "I never knew people of the home will acquire powers of some sort. They are alright." I move my head along to the song.

It mentions about books and instructions later in the song and recites the last verse, "They depend on me to save the home with objects, heroes, instructions and devices that will help defeat the ghost." I see Kiera and she wants to take the jugs. She tells me they want to see me in the office and she will do it for me. I nod as I trust her and head to the office.

I get there and look around. The phone rings at 9:30am. The building shakes. This voice says to see the window and jump into it. Then I hear something coming fast. I do as it says holding the phone in case. It gave me the word go and I stand on the desk. I see the thing jump into the window and land on the desk in the same spot as before. I leave and see phantoms going everywhere.

I spot Mia, Mark, Kiera, Stan, Sherry, and Charlette hanging in the Adult Room, having a discussion about a girl who has taken the 80s mix tape cassette player *Release The Ghost of hell'*. I stand there and admire the room. It's the same home as the one above; this is located underneath for people who passed away, known as the afterlife.

While looking, they mention our names. I find in the Adult Room all faces turned…asking to find me and I wave. Mia points saying, "I think she is here, Charlette." I turn around as well as my back was facing her. Charlette speaks loud and clear to me. I turn round and point at myself. "Yes, you," with the next command that made me shuffle forward.

As I approach the table, laying on there was a picture of a stone with a yellow glow. Black stone, red casing, heads for Earth, and also a statue in a theme park called something. The writing was covered by other papers on top so the name was not clear. The ghost. All look at me, Sherry, Mark, and Kiera. I lift my hands and show the device. They gasp as I explain to them the situation.

The ghosts were all quiet. Mia left the room with a devilish smile. Next was Sherry. She pat my shoulder but her hand went through. The rest look at me. As it was tense, I pull a chair, sit down and apply my manners. Charlette begins to speak.

"The device kept a ghost closed in another home. While the others move forward in time, it has been awakened by someone new and it continues to destroy everything in the home. We know it's the year 2036. Wiping out the humans in the home as of today."

My stomach shifts up and down with a nervous feeling. I look at them. A response comes, "You can stop this ghost by destroying the curse on the house before Halloween which is tomorrow." My eyes look at the table and there is a picture she points to. A photo of a blue light inside a white casing in memory in the home striking all my friends.

It takes Charlette off guard but still, she presses on with the rest of the information. "Another was a black light and red casing powers and these ones are somewhere in the world, blue is good, and black is well opposite of that." She throws the rest of the pictures and they scatter on the table in front of me. Also, there's a list of the different powers. The first one was change in skin tone, invisibility, laser, stretching parts, Fruit Stick, mind of knowledge, and last is the device.

Round one was with a question mark; no idea how it works. Next to it was the other list for the black casing and the six had different ones. I have a quick look at it as Charlette pushes me to the door. She tells me to listen to the Mix Tape for information and it also is the connection to them. I put that in the back of my mind and opened the Adult Room door leading to the Home 2036.

In Southampton Shopping Centre, Crazy Town. There are shops in the middle to look around and restaurants are located on the top where Lilly Pop and Janet Sweet are on work-related stuff as her daughter is somewhere else working. They go for food at a sandwich place named Bush Sandwich that sells sandwiches with meat and vegetarian, and also vegans. Suddenly, a black light with a red casing breaks the window, causing the glass to fly everywhere.

It hits Janet and Lily in the stomach but both of them are perfectly fine. Janet closes her eyes and the white light around her increases. The tables rise and fly at the person who is at the counter and they ducked under it. As it happens, there is a detective here. He came to take-away food from Hungry Hands which is next door to Bush Sandwich.

He spots both of them and gives the camera crew order to launch a live feed without getting close. There is a boy nearby and an object hits him right in the back and light surges through his body. The same happens to the lady in a red T-shirt with knee-length shorts. Something hit her i.e. four stones in one place. The two live here at Bush Sandwich and Hungry Hands. The camera continues to film and catches a dark spirit shooting right past down into the middle of the shopping centre.

The reporter says, "Where are the last two stones? We will never know. That is it from Kilo Alley News."

Chapter 4

London Piccadilly Circus Area News. Washington turns his computer on while watching gospel singing church on Whatch.online.com and enjoys his video. Something or someone is shocked by the banging on his door. He got a scare himself so he stops the video. This person, who is an article writer is in the building underneath and shows him a video.

The video was live two minutes ago because of the update to the media service. Washington watches that the girl has mind movement and the other woman has magic. The boy has black darts flying out and the last one was interesting. She creates a circle, annihilates the table, waves her hands and the circle disappears; then what happens is real.

After the circle is gone leaving the restaurants decimated into small piles of glass, the last thing this girl with mind does is make a circle and all jump through it. They could be anywhere in the world. I thank him for that as this gives me a case to investigate. There is a crash somewhere in the building, not in mine but it is another office.

The boy who showed me the video is still here and tells me it is Gwen's window. So, I shooed the guy who was about to speak and close the door. I jump into my chair, pick up the phone and dial Gwen's office. Seconds later, an answer comes that everything is fine.

Suddenly, she says, "Halloween Night, both worlds will be destroyed using a gate and the heroes of the Taunting Home will not stop." Her voice sounded odd. But I didn't get time to ask as her voice got back to normal, saying there will be someone coming from the newspaper building underneath. It is an intern and her name is Rose Billiard.

I put the phone down and the next thing there is a knock at the door. It is the intern and as I go to answer the door, she stands there smiling, ready to start a new job. This is who is sent to me by a detective in London. This person is very intelligent, smart, well-dressed, and his personality is nice. The phone on the desk pings loud enough for both of us to hear.

It reads: 'Washington, work with her or you lose your job. P.S. Find a story to impress me for the dinner party tomorrow night which happens to be Halloween Night.' I re-read the message and the girl starts asking about where can she sit, how things are running, and what story we will look into next.

"Be quiet please, I mean it." I point to a chair and she sits down and begins to hum in silence. I find my chair and spin. I bang my head on the desk. She makes sure I was fine; I lift my head and tell her it is okay. Rose takes the article and begins reading the story about Taunting Home which exploded by some purple light thirteen years ago.

It keeps her busy for a while. This is one hectic day, bombarded with tons of news. Taking one by one new intern makes you feel like a babysitter. The phone rings and I ignore it. The task is helping this girl sit there in front smiling. While pointing to the article, she babbles about the Care Home that was attacked by this purple light, bringing a curse where the ghost will rule both dimensions but the leader was imprisoned for thirteen years.

He was known as Empty ghost, which means the ghost was empty inside. It possessed Julie Kid Long who is now out; half her spirit is here in London to finish the task which is to rule the underworld located in Totland Bay. I look at her with surprise as she points to the article. This girl is clever.

She also tells me, "There is something else. It needs a gate opened to invade this home. She has ended up in London." Maybe this is the beginning of the partnership but still a little way to go. We both read the newspaper and it mentioned books and objects found in a Toyshop in Regent Street.

Rose and I walk out of the building. The train station is not too far and we get lovely sunshine. Rose is reading the paper. As we get there and search for the platform, a young boy walks past us reading a book and heading towards a book shop. I point in the direction as Rose turns to see the news building simmering in contrast to the building. It is hidden from human eyes and to us, it is the biggest book shop.

We get to the platform, hop on the train, and head to Oxford Circus. We get off there and walk up the stairs. As the train leaves, there is another sound in the tunnel but on the tabloid, it says one minute. This was no train at all. A voice echoes down the tunnel past the station and a wave of sonic sound breaks the tiles and makes the screen swing and heads to the tunnel. The people crouch on the floor.

Rose and I hear a message while covering our ears. "The ghost will begin the ceremony at 21:00pm and the end of the world you know it." I spot a girl standing there and she runs off. Tapping Rose's shoulder, we run after the girl. We get to the top but she is nowhere to be seen, but the Toyshop on Regent Street is nearby.

So, we walk down to find it. People are going in and out as we reach the entrance. It is stunning; amazing toys are everywhere on the five floors. We go to the escalator and head to the second floor. We waltz through things, and find toys, colourful pens, bouncy balls, controlled cars. A guy waves as he drives a car around and takes me by surprise.

Rose finds a marble size silver ball. My hand touches this meteor ball an there is yelling from downstairs from a young boy moving on the escalator. We duck out of sight and he scans with his black sunglasses. This is how we die…End of Washington.

I see Rose knocking a ball off the shelf and as it bounces, it increases in size. The boy spots her and fires little darts piercing the ball. Rose is fast. She picks a stick thinking it is a hammer and waves the thing. A light shoots out and makes it a hammer; it's created by thought and he swings this thing. I drop my meteor ball and it makes a hole, and an umbrella falls through the hole.

I see, next to Rose, the glowing light opens and the umbrellas fall to the ground, bounce and make a path going upwards. Rose jumps from one to another, heading higher. The light is gone and the ball is right in front of me. I laugh looking up and seeing her search for something. She grabs a blue ball. The boy laughs at her and he jumps on the stairs, blocking her way.

Taking chances here, she holds the ball and jumps with it, and creates a shield. She runs down the stairs and pushes the boy out of the way. Rose tells me to do what I did before. I grabbed the ball and dropped it while I thought of Lake Waves

Book Shop and she runs up to me. Her feet step over the hole and she is gone. I dive head first too, following her and trying not to lose her. The next few minutes are a blur.

We made it in the book shop called Lake Waves. It was just as big as River Stones. Outside the shop, Rose and I stood up and got our bearings before proceeding. She laughs and while managing a smile for her, I feel something like all along a friend.

Opening the doors, we both step inside. A waterfall is there and there is a bridge leading to the shop. Rose and I are handed a pair of glasses, both of us place them on and the entire bookshop emerges to life; there are tons of shelves of books. Rose points and I see a platform. I place my foot on and it takes us up and slides along to where the shelf said 'Teens' Books'.

I step off and Rose comes up after I land on the floor. We look and can see people underneath. We take the glasses off and there is nothing; all dark, empty void. We place them back on and the book shop was back in view. We walk along, searching for a book, and find fantasies vampires, action for teenagers, sci-fi, thrillers; classics were at the end, and history in the section straight ahead.

I walk while touching the shelves and Rose goes to the second floor above my head. I see stairs and run after her, stopping to a halt right in the middle of the path to see she has found a black book called *Sour Candy*. Rose opens a page and it shows us a map of the building, Taunting Home. It shows six dots moving around the home.

I look around to see if anyone else is there, Then a bang comes from below. I snap shut the book and give it to Rose. I nod to her to head towards the exit on my mark. It was the boy again with a tall, beautiful as Rose, woman. Rose was ready to run. The boy yells, "Ready!" The other two jump the corner and ambush us.

Walking backwards towards Rose, both of us meet in the middle before we think of a plan. I drop the ball thinking of downstairs and push Rose and she falls to the bottom. I grab a book and see the title, *Pop Sweet*. I open the cover and the boy fires black darts at me which makes me drop the book. I look at the page and a message soaked in ink spells the directions for another book named *Swinging Quirks* in another River Stones.

I expect this is in Southampton. It is our next destination. He moves closer with the woman pumping her fist to the floor and scorching all along until it reaches me. The two ladies from the right move like they are hunting their prey. I spot Rose underneath and she shows me the *Sour Candy* and blue Lego Instruction manual on how to build a portal.

She waves and I step my feet in the middle of the hole on the floor and free fall. I hit the floor as the hole closes. They scream. The boy and his companions turn the corner and see us. We run towards the exit. I pay for the book and as the receptionist gives me change, I thank them. Once out, we blink into the bright sunlight. Rose shows me the glasses.

"You stole them?" I ask.

"Borrowed them," she replies. We look at the manual instructions and press a button. Off it went and we see two young girls as two rocks, red and black, soar in the sky. We turned to leave, keeping hold of the *Sour Candy*. We open it and still, the red dots were in the home as we head to Southampton.

Chapter 5

10:25am, Care Home 2036

I manage to find everyone before it is too late. As I begin to talk, something hits the door. Every gut instinct of mine says to forget it. We stand in the middle as the door shakes more violently. This is the only time before anything happens. "You have powers." The door yanks open and it is home with no lights, all dark. A shadow crawls onto the floor, scratching it.

More come in as we move outside to Smoking Area in broad daylight. It still keeps intruding. We stop and hold our breath, hoping it retracts back to the home. I move forward to the door and try to keep them calm, telling them to stick with each other, and maybe lose the trolley for cleaning products and medication. All nod and go inside.

Cautiously I take each step and get to the door. I place one foot on the floor in the home and something felt cold which intrigues me. I'm doing this for friends. In the Activity Area, a white light appears with something like a pair of googles. I pick them up and put them on to see a book icon. I press that and now I'm holding the book for real.

I take the glasses off, now standing in darkness with a booklet of instructions on how to build a portal. Weird, glasses were gone.

I see a ghost smile. Her face contorts in anger and she roars *Sour Candy* and *Swinging Quirks*, and flies right at me. I fall backwards onto the floor. I sit there as the Activity Arena room lightens up brighter than before. Spotting the French doors, I walk through them. There is something that sits in the middle of the room next to a circle. The room was showing me information so I put the headphones on.

I see a ghost cutting the skin and blood pouring out the sides. It made me feel ill. The cut heals, as the circle glows but something is made of Lego. It can't be right. I remember the booklet. It is the gate. The ghost smiles, clicks her fingers and the room is empty. That is what going to happen. It is happy, it spins round doing a pirouette and jumps. Hands by the sides, it looks at us and laughs.

"Not long, Hannah, you won't be able to stop us. We will kill every human in the home, so you and the rest think you are superheroes of some sort," it sniggers. It produces a UNO Card which has number seven and the colour is green. It flicks at me and I dodged it. The card lands on the floor right at my feet. "You will not stop us, Hannah. One way or other, I will destroy the Home and you'll lose everything you know."

I pull the headphones off and before the room was breaking apart, I saw the letters 'JKL'. I made it out of the room and push the door, only to realise it is locked. I remember the code, 1764. The green light flashes and I push the bar and tumble forward. The black ink reaches me. The door was open and I turn to close it.

While sliding the door close, the shadow hooks the white painting on the door. I push it close and the ink squeals. It enters the home and I breathe. I walk around the corner to see them all together. The attacks are frequent as the day progress. It is just 11:00am.

The others are asking why we are outside. I give them a short explanation and point to the table. It is black and hot as well. He nods and points to my hand. He looks at the gloves, pulls the left hand off and touches it. His body turns black just like that and he smiles, clicks his fingers and makes a bat of black material.

We continue the list. Dixie breathes and builds her anger and her skin flickers as it camouflages in the surroundings, making her invisible. The third one is Paige. We all look at her and smile. We tell her to touch the table. "I'll do it with you." She nods and we raise our hands and place them. I let go and she is about to protest, so I quickly answer, "It burns my hand. Look it's all red," proving it did hurt.

She releases hers and there is nothing; *it is impossible.* Paige can touch hot things, also lasers. She press her wrist in her veins, made a hole…put on her eye as it fires laser inches from my head…release it from the eye to stop it. I look at Tillie. The sun is beating down on us. Lolly appears and tells me the letters mean a name. "I will share it later."

Lolly has mind powers. She closes her eyes as Gilberta is in front of us while we stand in the Taunting Home, showing us the Island Games with the letters written on the ground 'JKL' and opens them and all is gone. Tillie is impressed with all of them looking at the machine. I don't care as I trust her and hand her a cassette of 80s mix tape inside.

I already showed her the button to press and play the song that had beating drums and guitar intro. I tell her to look around. There is nothing but she spots something in the wall by the kitchen. Something pushing the wall. She takes the headphones off and points to the area. We go to look and discover it.

Chapter 6

We get to London's Waterloo big train station as the tabloid changes into numbers 21, 15, 14, and 7. Rose begins counting the alphabet in numbers and gets to the first one: 21 is T, O is 15, 14 is N and 7 is G. Once more the numbers 7, 8, 9, 21. "7 is G, 8 is H, 9 is I and the last one is 21, which is T, and that spells tonight."

I'm amazed by this as we have the word and we need to find a spell book. "May I speak, Washington? Let's try the book shop in Southampton, maybe the book is there." I point right at her good stood in the middle, and clack! Spread his arms to either side; the left goes up and the right down to the ground. Then it changes, the left-hand heads to the floor and the right up to the sky while laughing.

I also laugh walking towards him and giving a little push. He starts to move while laughing. I smile at him and we see a train leaving in three minutes from Platform 6. We head to the train and as we do, a boy runs into the station. The boy looks around panicked in my opinion and heads to us. "Rose Billiard, the intern at the Area News?"

What opening sentence is this? I follow with a 'yes' as my response. The boy talks about his nightmare which is real, explaining there is a book that allows the ghost to open a gate to both worlds. "Half of which is in the home and another set is somewhere. Don't let them use it. Once they do, can't help but for now, listen to me." I turn and see that the train is about to go.

"Thank you." He waves to us.

The boy is back with the two girls and the one that can do magic with her hands. What matters now is the train. Putting the book away, we run for the train and hop on as the train whistles. Nothing happens so we take seats and unwind. The train shutters forward. I look out of the window and there's nothing.

After two hours on the train, we get to Southampton Airport Parkway. The train stops and people pass-by. I spot the carriages and behind are the villains, walking closer and they see Washington and me. We are not far from Central when the first girl's skin starts glowing blue and yellow. The next one's face changes and her jawline moves as her teeth elongate into knives.

Her hands are spread apart and have seven fingers and toes as well. The girl turns and launches at me. The other one grips the table and makes a dent. She is strong, her muscles are pumping and a vein nearly burst. Her eyes enlarge and she yells, "This is not the end." Well, either one as she stands swings at Washington.

The bag is still with me which is holding the book of the Care Home. A person walks past us, nods and continues. She grabs my hands as I fall back onto the chairs with the table on the right and the other seats opposite. Washington punches the thing in the stomach. The Harley still standing throws her. She lands on the chairs opposite me.

Gripping the table and the chair above my head sliding back and forth, I throw at the first lady. She staggers backwards to the window where there are people sitting. The doors hissed open; trouble is coming.

The boy is here and the tall lady does magic. As she clicks her fingers, the windows on either side start ripping the train apart until the section where I'm standing. She rotates her fingers and the table slides right at me. I swing my hips smashing the lady with blue and yellow skin but she ducks under in time as the window smashed.

The boy asks for the location of the *Sour Candy*. Washington joins me behind as we move away. The window on the right rips open as we move at 100mph and see trees and tracks. She waves her hand and a light forms a circle that shoots along the carriage to the doors which are not far behind me. Washington pushes past me and begins to fight as the boy makes an introduction.

"This is Lauren, Lilly, and Janet. That is Harley and Daisy with yellow and blue skin. I am Quinn Stone." He nods and Janet, who was to the right, lifts a train track and slithers inside the carriage. I make a move towards the door as that distracted me (by the way, I am on a moving train, people, do not try this at all). Do not try this when travelling because I have great balance and so does Washington.

Quinn lifts his glasses and a dark blade from his eye comes forward. I feel for the ball in my pocket. Washington finds his. I pull a silver ball back into the toyshop. I turn it as the train slowly moves forward for me, heading to Airport Parkway. I let go and everything shifts back and the train is heading to Central as the dark blade from his eye shoots pointing to the door.

Washington moves and Janet stops, and using her mind, flicks the chair away and Lily fires a ball of magic at us. They approach us for the one thing they were after and ask about some books and gadgets the stone told each individual. Quinn touches Washington by the throat, lifting him gently; it was time to interject. "Hey! I know the book is not here so shove it in your throats."

The one who was magic hands lets go of Washington and comes towards me face to face. She laughs and turns her head to the top and all the others begin to laugh; I join as well. Janet moves as her hands pull as the light rips from the ceiling, hitting the floor right at my feet. Lauren fists her hands at the floor and aims at me. I walk forwards holding the bag with the book; it is safe as they didn't see it.

I answer, "Seriously, the book is somewhere else." I shrug my shoulders. Janet spins her fingers in a circle and makes a hole similar to Washington's with his ball. They join together and jump into nothingness. Lauren raises both hands and swings her wrist and the lights fade away as she disappears into the portal.

Washington and I could see passengers looking in disbelief as the train arrives at Southampton Central Station.

The next book is in River Stones. "Let's find it," I say as we get off the train.

Chapter 7

Washington and I walk to the shopping centre down the street. A car zooms by. Once inside, we see one person, Gwen, snooping and trying to find something and we hear her saying that another person is here stopping her from the future. She sends a group of high-skilled thief catchers of the time called The Bureau of Assassins in the future which sounds dangerous.

As she sees us, she marches up to greet us. Standing there, she talks about how she sold the building instantly and cameras are here. Before going, she tells us to not get involved with the Taunting Home problems before we get hurt. The voice changes and she says, "Get in the way and the consequences will be devasting for you and others around."

She reverts back to normal. Gwen shakes her head and tells us there is a party at Nation House in South Kensington at 21:00pm on Halloween Night. I keep my mouth shut until she leaves. "It is the same night for Taunting Home. We will get the book," Washington says and we both walk into the shop.

The time is 11:30am. He opens the book to see the red dots have moved; one is on Top Floor, two on the Middle, and one on Ground Floor. The house switches around while we watch. It was time to head down the escalator to the 'Teenager section'.

"The message said there is another one in there," Washington tells me. I see that we have arrived with books on the tables. One magically catches fire and burns away marking the table in charcoal. A message goes round then into the middle it read: DARE TO GO FURTHER AT YOUR RISK.

The message was clear. I tap Washington's shoulder to show him the writing on the books but it was not there. I swear I move away from him, jump up and down, place my hands on my head, screaming to the ceiling. I immediately look right at him, go around in a circle, stamp my feet, and hopscotch towards him as I point to the floor.

"Dare to go further at your risk." I manage to convince him and tried not to laugh. I stood there facing him and blowing hair out of my face smiling at him. We both laugh and walk further into the shop. There are more books on shelves and a wide table sits in front of us.

The wall shines black and the shadows creep along the shelves. We shuffle forward ignoring it. As we reach the end, there is a table with more books stacked in four piles, two on one side and the other two in piles behind. In the middle is a white panel saying: TURN BACK OR FACE THE HORROR.

We approach the table and it morphs away and a skeleton is dangling right in front of us. The chains snap and it falls, shattering to pieces. As the bones scatter, they build a bridge. Washington and I feel a chill down our spine while watching as a book flies off the shelf and smashes the bones. One of the pieces flies right at me.

Then a puppet or mannequin of some sort in a red jacket, that had strings to make it move, bangs the drums to the ballet piece of music *The Nutcracker* by Pyotr Ilyich Tchaikovsky as it march in our direction. Washington sees it too as it finishes. Music is coming from the speakers and I recognise it as the Russian dance from *The Nutcracker*.

The bones make a spider shape and jump onto Washington. I look at him and we both shrug our shoulders. The bone spider goes past. Then a black shape of a ghost appears. It reminds me of someone but the name is not coming. It whistles and books move.

Washington lets go of me and I fall to the floor and the books hit Washington. One hit me on the shoulder. The puppet was not behind me but it was right in my hands, screaming. The book knocks the puppet right out of my hands. The music gets louder and louder. I spot a book as it is shining in the light. I stare at it and another one whacks it, making it spin along the floor.

I catch a glimpse at the title: *Swinging Quirks*. Washington yells to grab it. I start chasing the book as another skeleton detaches from the wall and starts running. A spider and a skeleton head right at me and I dive for the book while Washington pulls the puppet away and throws it to the side. He sees a book and throws it.

The skeleton spider hits books on the left, sending books across the floor. The skeleton is still on my tail. I trip, sliding the rest of the way to the book. I grab it but now the skeleton is hovering inches away from me. It opens its jaw but Washington swings a book into its cranium and it falls next to me. While lying to breath, I see Washington smile and he gives me his hand to lift me up.

In the corner, the ghost was gone with dark shadows. The bookshop was normal and we were holding this piece.

Walking up the stairs back to the entrance, we see Quinn and his friends asking for the book. I shove it with *Sour Candy.*

At 12:30pm, back at the Care Home, Tillie shows where the dot was. All stand in the area waiting. Then it shifts again and there is something coming through. We ignore it for now as we eat. We found some pans and eggs in the fridge and made omelettes and pancakes. Also there is ham and cheese, butter and salmi to make sandwiches with leftovers.

As we eat, the radio plays a song, *Crazy Time,* and the intro rings through the kitchen. Tillie is happy; Richard is smirking; Lolly is grabbing things to begin cooking; Paige stands against the wall; Dixie gets involved in conversations; and as for me, I watch the day go by because it makes me feel happy. But a little tear falls down my cheek.

Lolly walks up to me and swings her hips as the song begins. She sings the first verse, "I walk into the building to work and look what I have found, ghosts want to tear the home apart taking another turn." It makes me laugh and I start to sway my hips too. Lolly looks at me and the rest shake their head.

"Putting pieces together makes us the better people, oh Crazy Time look at this, come on we can solve anything Crazy Time friendship is made along the way, we try too much just relax." They were impressed. Point to all of them as the chorus came again and all of us started singing while eating in between. "Lighting hits the Home now we have powers of our own, the evil spirit thinks we can't stop them take us there come on we can do it."

Paige spins in circles, Lolly jives, Richard twists his hands above his head and crosses his feet, and Tillie takes off the headphones to laugh and taps her feet. All breathe heavily. "Crazy Time fitting the puzzle together, Come on Crazy Time just a little Crazy Time taking day by day the ghost doesn't know us well just try friendship." Suddenly, the radio cracks.

All of us stop and we listen. It is sending a message to us, humans, to warn us that the dead will rule the Care Home and become the Queen of the underworld. The dead will celebrate and the ceremony will begin. It flicks again and resumes the song. I take a bite out of my omelette and others eat their sandwiches as we make the words of the song play.

In the last verse, we heard something that perks our interest. It went like this: "The ghost needs a gateway, but it needs jewels, can't seem to locate them, unless with the instructions. There is another book and Crazy Time piece of a puzzle, come on Crazy Time we stop the ghost from doing this. Crazy Time is the place to test our powers and make them understand, try a little more each time, this is Crazy Time."

I hear the voices of a man and a teenage girl speaking while others interfere with the signal. The clock strikes 13:00pm.

Chapter 8

I go outside to Smoking Area. Tillie and the rest come to see as the wall is fading. Tillie can see a door that I can't see. She walks right up to the wall and the bricks turn blue. The entire section clears as I approach. Tillie holds my hand. We go to the wall to see what is inside. For others, it was just bricks.

A creature jumps and pierces through, entering the home. We duck and the rest can see the wall turning clear and what have we done. Tillie and I go inside and the wall seals itself shut. Now it's just me and Tillie in this never-ending tunnel that is heading somewhere. Then images spit out as we walk down.

First one is of a girl who has a book, the friend has a medallion. Next, it's a boy with the same object, goggles which came here, and the name of the park and statues appears. Lastly was a man with yellow glasses who yells at us. All images fade away, leaving us in the car park of the Care Home. The wind blows showing that it is the year 2023.

How is that possible? We are from the year 2036. We step foot on the concrete floor and move carefully. Something moves in the home. A dark shadow is attacking the Middle Floor and I see Mark defending himself as the house shakes.

I watch as Tillie points up to the sky and it is blue light. Five seconds later, it hits us.

Stan is taking the bins out and as he sees us, he winks. Tillie and I run in his direction.

I begin with the tunnel in the Smoking Area and Tillie nods and tells him about the dark creature that enters our home in the future. Surprise is the expression on his face. "What do you mean?" It is hard to tell him that we are from thirteen years in the future. "I know you are from the Care Home above; also, the year is 2036 up there. Back on the topic at hand, how did it escape? Did you press a hand on the wall?"

Tillie nods in disappointment. He sighs. It kills your friends and the only one thing, that is a fruit stick, allows the person to access power and also stop the ghost from the other world. I knew the answer. "Stan, it is in UK somewhere but we have no idea yet."

"Thank you both. You get out before it is late." He turns. The dark shadow from the building hears the voice from the Care Home. The plan was to build anger in Tillie and make her hate me and later take the blame.

"It is your fault; this is your doing!"

She goes red and answers, "What did you say?" I repeat the sentence and she gets angry and the white light pulses around her.

I take her hands and point at the creature, whispering, "This is our problem." I hit her on the cheek, tipping her off. She yells and the light fires at the home. Stan grabs me and Tillie flies to the ceiling. I let go of Tillie and place her hand above her head. The door opens and we go right through the end and we are back at the Home at 13:30pm.

My mind finds out there is another object. Also, time is ten minutes faster Underground.

The Home is turning. I open the door and go in to reach for Tillie but she wants to be alone. I say I am sorry before closing the door. The stairs have vines slithering down the rails and walking up those stairs feels like walking in an overgrown garden that needs cutting. I reach the gate and push it open.

I step on the floor and voices come from the Middle Floor. The floor I land on is Top Floor. I spot a room and once my foot goes past the door frame, the bathroom is on the right as is the toilet. On the wall, there is black ink and it pops onto the seat as it makes a wasp head. It moves and the rest of the body is forming.

Stepping backwards into the hallway, I see the door on the left swing open and ink shoots out, hitting the wall. I stumble deeper down the corridor as the room straightens. The creature melts into little ink blobs like ants that form a human body. I crouch, never taking my eyes off it. I grab the stomach as more ants crawl inside as it still builds the shape.

This figure flexes the biceps and with the other hand reaches and pulls the bone, and yanks it out of the ants moving everywhere. I felt little that one was real eye as rolling it came to me. I'm about to vomit and the legs shiver. The kneecap shoots forward in the centre snaps, the head bends backwards to the ceiling, and black liquid shoots to the ceiling, sticking in the room.

On the left, a hand sticks out with sharp nails scratching the wall. It pulls and more of the arm comes into view; the body is not there; it is now in the hallway marching towards me. I scramble backwards, telling myself 'I have friends'. The ink stops moving…

…Silence. Then the eye explodes and goes on the walls. This black ink takes one step forward but the foot gets stuck in. It merges together, making another shape of a ball. The bathroom door flings open. It was the ghost. It smiles at me and says, "Think you can stop me?" It goes to reach me. I tell it that I have friends and it screams very loudly that it echoes.

While covering my ears, I sit back against the wall. The sink pings and the ghost goes through its body. The pipe breaks and water showers in there, making a puddle. I say it one more time and the ghost yells and the bath shatters into pieces. Water spills into the hallway.

I see a picture on the wall of letters. As it swings upside down, the letters form JKL. The next one is rocking left to right and it was of all the carers—Mark, Mia, Sherry, Stan, Kiera, and Charlette. But the one on the right was her. It fell and the eye is growing in size as big as a basketball. I watch the puddle as it reflects something.

I lean forward to see something and go to grab it. The ball bounces and flies, and the ink jerks forward. I shove my hand in the puddle and it goes through. The stick made an umbrella covering me as the blood went to the left and right. I get up and footsteps are coming up. The ink spilled away further into the home. I see Lolly and the others. "Tillie is not here?"

"She is safe in the Adult Room." I look at the watch the time is now 13:50pm in the building. We all walk down to the room to see Tillie upset, listening to *Breaking People's heart in pieces.* "I get the cassette with the tape it was cool, nothing stopping me from saying things to hurt others because I break people's hearts in pieces, I do something which leads to the gates of hell and bring bad luck to my friends how are nice because I break people's heart in pieces."

We all come in and sit at the table while she sings. It is impressive as she has a lovely voice. She whips the headphones off in surprise and wipes her tears away. Not a problem for us; we all nod. Tillie smiles.

Lolly's eyes shine and she breathes hard as another vision happens. This one is a theme-park. The name we've established inside this park is a café named Chatty Chills. In here is a lady who is round, strong and dark-skinned, needs glasses to read things, with another lady in chill clothes— clotted trousers, a black top, and hair in a pony tail, she watches a device which allows something to happen.

The lady opposite says she needs a stone from Amsterdam; blue was the colour. As the vision is finishing, purple light lights the sky.

We run as they fire upon us and push a table towards them, sliding head first with the table and taking the force. Washington drops the ball and thinks of outside of the shopping centre. He steps and he is now outside. He runs back in to meet me. I smile and shrug. As we run into the centre, a girl bumps on the way and spots the squad watching.

This person steals the keys to the car, hops in and jumps the engine off. They follow and the others fire at us. We head past a restaurant called Jelly Atlas where the tables were made of jelly. Also, the decorations inside too, and the menu is written in jelly. Now I remember in the bag is the book, *Sour Candy*. All the dots are moving the Home and I turn the page to see a map of the shopping centre.

Then a black dart skims my ear and I turn to see them behind me, gaining fast. Washington sees the stairs and says to go up. I follow the instructions and he clicks his knuckles ready to fight. The boy first punches him in the stomach, then the side. He goes down and does a kick and begins to run for the stairs. Next is the magic one who rips the railing, flinging metal screws, breaking glass, making it difficult to climb.

After this is the mind one who stops. Washington begins to slow down as he is a big fella but it will take more than this to physically slow the momentum to a complete halt; the lady with red dark magic creates a red circle. As it shoots upwards, the path is gone. I make it to the top. The girl with the skin colour of yellow, green, and blue jumps onto the railing.

She again lands face-to-face with me. I swing and dodge, kicking at her shin which makes her fall. The last person jumps and lands behind Washington. A plan forms in my head. I kick the girl and dodge her as we run to the shop.

While running, Janet here throws the glass panels onto the path, timing each one as they smash into the shop behind us and it continues to my surprise. Washington halts as Lilly fires a ball. He loses his balance and tumbles into a shop. He is still okay and I turn to see her laughing. It was time.

I got my silver ball and spin it. Washington runs backwards a few seconds before the shop. I stop, let go and it reruns the whole minute. I grab him and we both jump to the ground as Lilly's fires miss us. We stumble a little heading into a shop called Bold Bags. The shop sells bags from big brands to descents ones.

We hid in there and Washington drops the ball. It hits him in the face and I tell him to get his act together before getting injured. He shakes his head and thinks of the Cruise Terminal in Southampton. We fall through the empty void into a cloudless sky with hot beating sun nearly blinding us.

Chapter 9

We made it landing in a taxi rank for cars to see people taking luggage to conveyor belts to be sent on the ship. We run across as his hole closes and the ball falls from the sky. He catches and it shows the thing to me as I wave to come. Inside is large a waiting room with seats all along both sides.

There is a counter with a huge screen to protect them. We watch a boy run in our direction. He was the one from the train station. He greets us and we look at him. He tells the ticket office we are his family and points to the ticket. We understand and he tells us to move. We do as told. Washington peers over his shoulder and thinks he is safe.

We pass a lot of people and get on the ship. We find the rooms and he tells ours is here and he is in the next one. So, we close the door. Washington and I decide to explore first and we do a fire drill before anything happens. The group will not look here for us. I try unwinding my mind and head to the area.

John points to a map showing the places and mentions a ballroom. It piques interest in Washington so we will do this after the fire drill which is fine with him.

14:30pm at the Care Home, a purple light spreads across the Home. We hear a loud noise from upstairs and I tell them it wants all of us. Richard says, "Staying behind you just in case." There's no arguing. The table moves and all of us grab something.

We proceed to the door and the noise gets louder and louder. As I go to step inside, the door slams shut. All are in the room but me. I yell and hit the door, it wasn't fair. Lolly says to come with her and all go. no idea. The noise bounces off the walls and echoes down relentlessly. Stepping on, the stairs come into view but which way to go?

The Middle is at the bottom; Top is in the middle so it means I have to head to the top. I walk up the stairs to the Top and the door is covered in black ink. I press the handle so hard that the door flings off its hinges. I step past it and look everywhere. The sound is still here with me while I hold this Fruit Stick.

The light above me is flicking on and off. The pictures are about to fall off the wall and the wallpaper is stripping away, showing the Home colliding with reality and pushing on. I march down this hallway in half-light and darkness. The stairs are on the left of me as a loud noise comes from upstairs, indicating the Ground Floor waling up. The noise is growing there and I move the Fruit Stick above my head. It glows and then nothing…

It is absolutely silent as the night. Something falls before my feet and I search around. I see dark red blood on the ceiling and there's an eye with a needle poked through it, blood dripping from it. The kitchen is here and the door is fine. On the right is another one to the bathroom which creaks open.

A hand creeps over the edge, not showing much. The skin is yellow and it glows in the room. The light is bright and the florescent lights breaks. The corridor is dark as night. I feel getting sucked into a void. I try to hold the Fruit Stick but the thing is not there. The trolley is out and a bang! I point to the trolley and see that the tea trolley has a red liquid spilled across the top.

It turns out to be a human with the liver ripped open. A creature spins round to face me. The creature is 5 foot 6 inches tall, has black skin, scales, a glint in its light, eyes as a serpent, teeth were curved, and hands have sharp nails which could scratch easily. My legs had goosebumps all the way down; it was enough to see the body. This means I could see the skeleton system underneath it.

It screeched out in a loud whisper, "The ghost of the dead is awake and time is coming to end both the worlds. The Care Home will suffer till the dead rule!" I watch this creature and it jumps right at me. It grabs me by my shoulders and its tongue falls out of the mouth, slick as oil, and begins to lick my face like a dog that is happy to see you. It licks again and those sharp nails press against my skin.

The tongue slides back in its mouth and then it's gone. I shine the light but it was not there anymore. To my surprise, I see my friends in the corridor in full light. The trolley is gone. It was like I'm losing my mind. It's time we put pieces of the puzzle together. We all nod.

Every time all of us step in the Home, it tries to separate us and these things make images. The team should stay together and everyone shakes heads in agreement. It's time to end the disaster.

Chapter 10

Washington, John and I walk out of the bar and I see people with headsets looking for someone. It doesn't matter to us as we are here not to think about anyone else. We sail to Bruges and all of us walk past a café and see a waiter. On the tray is a gem. It is yellow. We should come back for this.

We head outside to the deck. On the way as we got in the lift, Washington tells us that he will be in the ballroom. We head up. The lift slows down but we haven't reached the floor. John covers his ears as a loud vibration against the door comes inside. He makes me copy him.

It shouts, "The ghost will have control; stand back, the dark spirit is here," and laughs away into emptiness. The lift kicks into motion again and we make it to the deck eventually. We look around and it is sunny outside, and we see people having fun. I text Washington and get a response saying he is fine.

We stroll down the deck with the swimming pool. On the right, there is a girl running on top with people following behind, they were jumping and firing. Suddenly, the day is out of sync which is not relaxing but I keep calm.

John and I walk round the ship to the back. We go up the stairs. I keep the books with me at all times. I open the *Sour*

Candy and John's eyes could see the writing. He tells me, "Today it a celebration of the undead, rise of the spirit. Welcome back and throwing a party at 21:00pm."

John stops and we both know what that means. Both homes are beginning to get destroyed soon and wants help. He goes upstairs leaving me alone. The stairs shine a colour, blue and yellow, but the Home is Totland. I place a foot on the step and the reflection spreads to the wall.

I see all six heroes talking about how they have objects and to throw a celebration in their home with a gate. I remember Gwen saying to not try. Washington is in the ballroom but I open the book standing there and see the dots. They are real people but the image fades and the last thing shown is JKL. I will not stop this team of heroes and stand back on the cruise. I turn to locate the ballroom at the front, it is time to join Washington.

Care Home 21:00pm: The night before Halloween, all of us are here alive. We manage to get the letters 'J, K, L' which means a name. I was shown the Activity Arena, which is the place; the Lego booklet is the gate. All these things are there for a reason. Tillie listens and we hear voices from the ghost in the Home 2023. Everyone is fine but Lolly begins to glow.

I grab her shoulder and Richard is on the other side. Paige holds the waist, Tillie the hips, and Dixie the arm. Everything around me changes but we all breathe in relief. Lolly screams as we all land on tables and chairs. Richard hits the floor which wasn't wooden. The lockers remind of a dinner restaurant. The ship moves left to right and I spot the name called 'Ballroom Diner'.

It is night time and it's empty, just us in here. I see in the middle of a room there is a stage naming each dish and on the other side is a ballroom card with ten ballroom dances—waltz, Viennese Waltz, Quick step, Jive, Charleston, Tango, Argentine Tango, Rhumba, Cha-cha, and Samba. It has pictures to show which one is which.

The first one is a waltz, showing a spinning position and it was like that for the other dances. Along the wall were feet showing the opening of the dance. Feet were apart for Waltz; straight legs for Cha-cha and Samba has width apart, shaking hips, rotating and bent in the air; the other is straight for Charleston; flick and kick for Jive. It is amazing.

Then the doors open and a sound echoes. In front of us is a man who drops a ball and whistles to follow. They run towards it but as we get there, he is gone, The hole is still open and I shove Richard, Lolly, Dixie, wherever she might be Paige and Tillie, and finally, I pull the Fruit Stick and press a button, making a shield. I fall through and end up on a deck with a swimming pool on the right.

The stars glow in the bright sky. We all stand there in shock. He looks at us and then back to the starry sky. There is a young girl in her twenties retracing her steps along the deck with a torch and behind her are some people chasing her. She comes down the stairs and creates a blue circle and off she goes somewhere.

I remember, a voice said: Washington. The man, hears and looks at me. "Hannah from Taunting Home." He smiles, the young girl joins us asking him thanks. He explains we are the heroes of Taunting Home. Paige takes my hand and closes her eyes. My clothes begin to change to a knee-length summer dress with flowers and my hair is in a French plait.

It is a new look for me and the others smile. Washington shakes my hand and Rose smiles in fascination. She stops what she is doing and I spin. It lights up the sky and all laugh. Jazz music plays from the speakers in the distance. As the song begins, Washington teaches me how to dance. All of us copy.

Rose seemed nervous so Paige takes her hand and yanks her along. We stand side by side as Washington is in his element of dance. The music continues and as the song starts, he sings to it. "I don't know how but it is easy, 1,2,3 but I can dance, finding objects all the place but I can dance." Rose slides past us to the front. The second verse is quick. "I found things I never would, books that have magic but I can dance."

Washington's voice sings loudly, "Look at both of us here on a cruise, saving the home and will do anything to help, also people want the objects to destroy the world but it won't happen, while we wait, enjoy the moment and I can dance." Paige and I spin in a circle and tap our feet up and down clicking our fingers. Richard swings his hands, twisting his hips along with Washington. Rose and Tillie hold hands and lift their feet in sync. The music stops as the speaker breaks.

We all turn round to see a group of people like us who have some sort of power. "Enjoying the cruise, Washington." The expression changes on their faces. They all ask for gems and we have no idea. The boy sees me in my dress. The stare is like ice-cold daggers to the heart. He fires a dart at the floor, missing us. We have a head-start and we take advantage of it.

Lauren points to the rest of us and we all nod and spring into action. We head to the bar and it rocks to the right. We miss it. The buffet is inside so the rest follow behind. Janet moves the table and smashes it into a bar, causing a fire. Lauren's wrist is alight. She yells and slams her hand into the board and a black mark slides along the bar.

It makes us go into the buffet area. The time is 21:15pm. Once inside, we go straight on and out the other side. They blow the glass door off its hinges and we hide. Daisy is here walking and Harley is next to her. On the other side are Lauren, Janet, and Lilly. Quinn is following behind and his mind is flicking.

Moonlight shines, leading the way and we run towards the exit. I hear a noise of something moving but none of us are. Washington points out that it is Harley on the tables, scratching as she moves. Daisy is humming for the others. It is okay. We wait in silence which gets stretched out to minutes. The cruise shakes and cups fall, creating a loud noise.

Daisy and Harley move in seconds, and we all get up and move towards the exit. A black dart hits the wooden floor next to me. Quinn looks at me and his lips whisper, "Run." I do not trust him but I have no choice. So, I get the group and we start to run. He attacks the kitchen and the others jump to the sound. As we reach the exit, he smiles at me in a friendly way.

We make it outside and all are breathing heavily. Light is still glowing above our heads. Quinn walks out and Washington picks him up. There's no reaction time for an explanation. While Washington holds him, he laughs a little As his chest tightens, he begins to tell us about the home. We need gems to destroy both homes.

He wants to be a good person and do something right because in his mind, choosing villainy is not his fault. The sound is closing the distance. Washington puts him down with a death stare. Quinn nods and walks back into the buffet. "I am sorry, only want to try to be good," he tells the others. Nothing goes away, all sigh.

The room goes quiet. The rooms are two flights of stairs down. As we are about to go down, outside we all hear, "A boy is cursed until 24 December." We head to rooms. Once outside the cabin doors, Rose points to hers and Washington says he is there and that one is of the boy who let us on.

I don't ask and waltz in. I make sleeping arrangements. The bed is for Rose who instead wants to sleep in the chair; the stool with the mirror was for Paige who closes her eyes slowly; the bed was for Tillie. I turn the light off and go to sleep.

Chapter 11

Amsterdam, 08:00am, Halloween Night

The bell rings and the announcer is making a speech, saying that we have arrived at Amsterdam. The sound wakes me up. Also, I am an early riser so I am used to it. I search for the stick on the bedside table and head to the mirror. I press a button, the white one spins the circle and my clothes change into shorts, a t-shirt with flowers of pretty colours, and a ponytail hairstyle. While admiring the look, I see Paige asleep and the others were still asleep too.

I hear a knock and go to see. It is Washington and Richard. The boys are all ready for the day. I release the hatch on the door open and let them in. Washington comments on the way I look and whistles. Washington takes the ball and squeezes it which makes a loud sound. Paige sits up. Tillie sits up bolt right. Rose startles in the chair and notices we are ready to leave.

Washington is here and she blushes. We all laugh and get up to talk about today. All get dressed and have breakfast. The plan is to explore the city. We head to the exit on the side. Feeling feet on the ground and not the carpet all the time is different. There's lovely sunshine, grey but warm. The wind is cold but not a problem for us. We walk into the centre where boats are sailing down the river.

We reach the centre and a shop has jewels. There is a red one that is shining bright. After looking around, Rose goes inside and comes back with the red jewel. She loves it. So I get the stick out, it glows with the gentle press and changes into the camera. We take a photo. Something is here above the building but we can see nothing. We have had enough of Taunting Home. It was a change of scenery we needed.

Still, the camera keeps operating. It is a person moving. Afterwards, I turn it off. Rose says, "You should wear it because looks good on you." On the stick, I find a green button and press down. The thing scans over the jewel and transfers it to your hand as a duplicate.

"You wear it as a necklace." Rose holds the real gem and smiles to see that I have the gem in a necklace which is a duplicate. The time is one hour ahead so it is 08:20am.

I walk along a path that has houses, water flowing under a bridge, and going to the other side. Paige calls my name and I turn to see her feet slowly dragging. Richard was losing his hands as they were vanishing. We have to get back to the Home immediately. I hurry along the path up to Washington and Rose and tell them everything about getting back to the Home.

Both are understanding people. A train comes into view and it passes right in the middle of the road. The second one comes and it breaks off the tracks, nearly hitting everyone. Rose pulls her silver ball and turns it. The train goes backwards and we can all see that it is amazing.

Rose shoves us one by one across the street as the train breaks off the tracks again and misses us. Time has caught up.

That was quick. Before going back, they mention a stone, Emerald coloured, in the flower café.

Back at the cruise ship, we walk up the deck and find the café. We see a waiter carrying a silver tray and inside was the gem. It is time to get it. Washington shakes his ball and it flies up and lands next to the waiter. The tray moves down then back up. He manages to grab the gem and show us.

I feel something go past me quick as a blur. It is Harley. She runs and jumps. Washington drops the ball which makes a hole He drops the gem and I see a light and the exit. Rose runs to it as a blue ball hits and explodes in front of her. For a second, we are blinded and I tell the rest to get the gem and head to the buffet area. All of us begin to chase the gem.

I whistle and the floor changes to glass all along. I do it again and the rail swings off and slams into the girl with magic. Something inside me feels strange. I click my fingers and throw UNO cards at them. She laughs and runs towards me but the cards blow up with each throw.

Tillie sings and white bright light fires out breaking the glass floor I created. I jump over and tell her it is fine. "Paige!" She turns. She now puts both her hands together and heat burns from them. She separates them and light fires from the centre of her palms. Richard touches the rail and his body changes colour. He makes a disc and throws it. Janet gets hit.

Quinn hits Washington in the stomach and says to him, "Go, I hold them off okay." Washington gets stunned by his words but just does it. He runs and drops his ball, making a hole. He heads to the thing with the gem and jumps over the railing. Richard makes a slide and he lands.

He turns and his skin changes as he loses more of his hand to the body. Rose is there and she jumps. Tillie sings and a white light makes a trampoline for Rose and she bounces to safety. She gets the gem and goes through the hole into bright white light.

We make it on the deck as Paige's legs are disappearing. The thing is getting worse. We find the swimming pool. Paige grabs my hand and my clothes change into a swimming costume of a pink bikini which has yellow dots and palm trees. I dive into the water as others hold Paige's hand one at a time. First is Richard who has red swimming shorts; next is Lolly with a black bra and knickers, her hair flutters in the wind.

After that, Tillie gets a swimsuit of a light blue colour bra and the bottom half of same colour. She also has a camera with a glistening shine; and finally, it's Dixie who has a yellow bra with white dots and the bottom half had the same pattern. We all dive into the water and watch Washington and Rose fight to save us. winks at me and we all dive underwater.

As we swim to the ground, suddenly a white light glows across the surface. Another swimmer joins us; it was Quinn. I touch the light and my hand feels a tingle of electricity flowing through my body. I swing my head to send a signal as the light fades. I swim and pull Richard's arm and point thrusting my hand to the floor.

He sees and I push him, Lolly follows and next is Tillie. The glistening shine was a waterproof device. Dixie goes and then lastly it is me. Like a train heading to the station. This boy is a fast swimmer and he quickens his pace to catch up. Everyone is gone which makes no sense.

As I reach the light, my hand phases in and out of it. I crawl up. The boy is close and he points to the surface then himself and then right at me. In my mind, I think the boy wants to be good. I return a sign and point myself then at him. He nods as a red light glows on the surface. I think about Washington.

I tread water as the light is fading quickly. The boy signs okay and swims upwards to the surface. The light is closing and my thoughts are scrambled at that moment. I stretch out my hand which goes through, then the body and I close my eyes…

Bang! My head hits the post of a table. I rub where it hurts and look up to see all of them happy. Paige sits next to me making sure I was okay. This made me realise the key to saving this Care Home is friendship.

Chapter 12

Tillie says she went into the kitchen and found a gem, She comes back and it is a yellow gem. I have the red gem round my neck. The light is closes something to happen silence Paige is next to me on the floor, talking things out but it is not helping. There is nothing we can do at the moment as the time is 07:40 am. Richard picks up the remote for the TV and puts it on.

News headlines flash that Gwen Harmony is hosting a party tonight a Nation Party. Dixie is human and she sits watching it. Then her attention diverts to the fridge. She opens it and a ball falls out. She picks it up and it glows brightly. She places it with the gems. Tillie presses the rewind button on the mix tape machine and sings the song, "Different Home will collide as the ghost will rule. The party is at nine o'clock and Julie Kid Long gets her revenge."

In my mind, the name is ringing hums. I tell them about the accident in 2023. I point to the paper and every person peers at the headline—*Freak accident at the Care Home.* Tillie sings, "Lego instructions will build the gate, this is how we stop her." The light shines when we read her name, JULIE KID LONG, written in capital letters. We all are shocked and the building is swapping. It is 08:00am.

Paige is going to the Dinner Area to use her powers and Lolly will go on a floor. Dixie has the Wing together with Tillie, the Middle was Lolly, and Richard which means the Bottom is Paige. I share about the theme park which is called 'The Last Action Adventure Centre'. Also, the camp is attacked by a guy who calls himself the Smiler. We have no idea how he disappeared from the world.

The TV mentions a rock that has divine powers and it has landed in a country side in UK. The statute is tall, has a small square base. The studio shows a picture of the boy on the cruise having nightmares that become real. Then it goes live to the terminal in Southampton and Washington and Rose are speaking. They say there is a party tonight and that Gwen is paying a millionaire for the News Article.

Finally, news mentions a church in the South of France splitting a medallion into three pieces across Europe. It hit me that this is bigger than ever.

The six of us really talk then and go to our separate rooms to practice training before the party. I go to the Ground in the Diner Area with Paige full of excitement. I get inside and we start whistling. As she does, a light came out of her palm and she fires at the ceiling and the chandelier wobbles left and right. Whipping the Fruit Stick out, I press the red button and point at the thing.

Breathing in and out, holding the stick, the object places itself back in the original place but in my mind, I have a different tactic. I put my hands together and slap it so hard, it leaves a mark. She breathes and the hand vibrates. I go to slap again but it passes through. My eyes follow the sensation. I slap once more but it goes through her hands completely.

Paige stops breathing and her hands revert to normal state. It was good. She whistles and ducks down and instead points at the reflecting glass on the other side, herself moved aside the table. Stops again. Laughing, she joins in and goes back to try in. Huffing, I helped her…She points to the Fruit Stick. Now it is my turn.

I press the green one and the first object glows. I click again and the chair grows in size; I spin a circle and it changes to duplicate. Now there are two chairs. I change it to the blue button and the table shines bright. I press the button and it disappears and reappears seconds later. Paige is amazed. I press the buttons and everything is back to how it was.

I tell her that I will see the others for a minute so she practices on aiming. I head to the Middle Floor which is at the Top as the floor has been swapped.

Once there, I see Lolly and Richard messing around throwing things. I see Lolly running so quickly that it was a blur. She stops in front of me. Richard breathes deeply and his legs start sinking through the carpet and his hands press on the floor to lift himself like he was exercising, doing triceps. They were fine so I walk away waving to them. Both wave back and continue with the task.

I lastly go up the stairs to Wing to see Dixie and Tillie. I see everyone is working together but I feel something in my stomach to be in charge of all this. I see Tillie hums and the machine keeps singing and a white light fires out, slicing the walls. It is not loud enough to destroy anything. As for Dixie, she screams and a circle comes towards me.

It dies down and her screaming slows to a halt. She spots me standing there and comes up to greet me. I wave off as I didn't want to disturb what they were doing. "Explain what is happening." Dixie tells the ball needs an energy source. I look at Tillie and ask to give it to her. Dixie hands her the ball. "Look after it." She smiles, and we laugh.

It was time to end the reign of the evil spirit.

Chapter 13

It is 08:40am. Washington and I are on the cruise ship and I find his book and put it in my bag with the addition of the glasses that are somewhere in Europe. We exit after giving an interview to the news reporters and looking past them, I see the boy who came running to us. The same one who happened to be on the two-day cruise and the exact same one who knows stuff about Hannah and her friends.

I spot him getting in a taxi and going to the train station and I guess we'll never see him again. Minutes later, another one joins us. The boy is wearing a black drench coat and glasses. Keeping safe from the eyes of people, I hold the book called *Sour Candy,* and Washington has *Swinging Quirks,* which has the location of Hannah.

This boy spoke like he was out of breath and explains that he wants to help and be a good person. "Hannah understood what I said. They will destroy both homes and a quarter of Totland on the Isle of Wight is going to be gone. Gwen paid a person who is rich to take over the News Article. Tonight is the Halloween Party at 21:00pm."

I thank him and he shakes my hand. He disappears before the others join and off they go to London. Washington and I stand in amazement with this information. We also have to go to London. Washington shakes his meteor ball and it vibrates. He throws it a few feet in front of us and it transforms into a Cadillac playing 80s song guitar intro.

"Time to stop the party and the ghost will see heroes can put an end to this. Head to London for a party, let's do this. Solve the mystery come on, find all the answers, solve the mystery, help our friends." He gestures to me to get in the car which I do. I run round the car touching the bumper on the front of the hood and watching that he is fit and strong.

He opens the door and then spots there's no wheel. How on earth are we going to drive? The door closes and something glows in front of us. It is Lauren with her red circles power which left destruction on the cruise. Washington turns the knob on the radio station and a 1950s style of music is playing. "Everybody is somebody fool Connie Francis."

The car moves at the normal speed of 40mph leaving the terminal and heading to London. I listen to the song and realise it is a great song. I even sing along while driving through Southampton, heading to the motorway. There is crackling in the background.

It is 09:00am. The Wing and the Activity Area move around. Now left are the rooms and right is the Activity Area. We wait for it to finish and make sense. Richard says he found the clue about the boy who had dreams that were real. I missed that. He is right, I need his help. I am pushing him away and the only hope is doing it together but I can't lose any one. Lolly says, "Don't get mad about her not finding clues."

Richard says, "Pushing us to the side to make sure we are safe but what about yourself? This is about everybody's safety. I mean it in the nicest possible way, take our help. I'll find some in the house and we'll come back here and solve the puzzle." He walks out of the room. Lolly tries to say something but I wave her off okay. She stands there feeling upset.

Paige is next to say, "I will head straight here if anything goes sideways. He needs time to find clues and might realise he needs your help." She steps past me and heads to the Middle Floor. Dixie walks to the Top Floor without saying a word.

Tillie says, "Something is cracking on my machine and I'm hearing a song. Also, voices driving along a road." I leave the room and stand-alone. Little tears fall and anger builds up inside me but I keep calm by telling myself I can do this with their help. The lockers shake and make me jump. Water turns on in the sink and it pours out but it changes to blood and splatters. Something is happening.

I wait and the blood stops. The tables slide towards the lockers. I jump onto the table and then slide off to the side into the door leading to the Wing. I make a left and it is the Activity Area. A card is on the floor; a UNO card. Another trial along to the French doors, step past each, I count down from five to one. At the end is a wild card. I make it to the doors to see a grand white light in the middle of the room.

Something or someone sits there chanting. I shuffle my feet closer and it turns head with a snapping sound. The thing faces me for a brief second. It has two heads, one eye, six arms, and four legs. I'm jolted forward as I'm frozen to the spot. I scream loudly but it comes and fades into smoke. I try to catch my breathing next.

It is a ghost; the one who has been trapped for thirteen years. The ghost not to be mentioned caused the freak accident. Sound echoes down to the end and the thing spins round to see me laugh and tell myself it is not there. It mocks me, "Not there?" The ghost dances up to me. I open my eyes and it is right in my face.

It yells, "Really?" I stumble backwards and scramble away. I get to my feet and before leaving I see a gate in the middle that waves to me and flashes Lego pieces. The instructions booklet needs to get to others.

It is 9:10 am. I make it to the floor. On the right of it, there are three big floors Top, Middle and Ground. I run to the board that hangs on the wall at the end. Suddenly, a hand bursts out of the wallpaper. I stop and my feet burn as I skid to a halt but not slow enough. The railing which sits there is gone straight into the abyss of nothingness.

As it recloses itself, the hand swings round about to hit me. Now floating, I land on a path that leads to the right. I turn the corner and down this hallway, above me is the home from 2036, and underneath is the home in the year 2023. While running down the path, I see sunshine gaining divine powers.

Later on a robot from the future, then the image shifts and there are three young people who have a medallion each; children with wrist watches in the park; a boy and girl facing nightmares; five in a science lab control experiment; a creature from the lab; a boy changing colours; also, a train that can talk in a house with a little man driving; then a girl named Dorthey.

Finally, it is a person that madly laughs. I move forward and just after that, near the end, the girl is in London looking for a book. It also shows the future of that place. There is a man who goes by the name D-Man. Next it is the girl and Prime Frost in a Ferrari sports car driving to Newport of 2038.

"Let's find the children with the watches or the park will crumble. Are we clear?"

"Yes," replies Daisy in clotted trousers with red and white dot pattern and has a gold bracelet, also earrings to match. The vision is gone and I see Richard. My wrist watch says 09:30am where I was standing. I look up as Richard moves and see the room change to dolls and books. The time is 09:20am. It is scary time moves fast.

Just behind me Sherry and she comes right at me. I dive forward with the Fruit Stick. Sherry misses me and I stand up. The path is nearly coming to the end of the line and I run the last few steps. The bright white light is gone and I enter a room in total darkness. I hear something and it moves at my feet. I shake my hand with the Fruit Stick and a light comes on.

I look at the watch and it reads 09:30am. I turn to see a poster on the wall of a horror film. Next to it was a doll made of soft fabric and has white teeth which are grinding. As it opens, inside is a dark green substance that is fired at me. I duck under it but it falls on the floor and melts the floorboards. I stare at the doll and pull the handle. It was soft.

It is an awful feeling when I look at it and realise it is an intestine from the human body. I yank it open and step through, nearly vomiting. Richard and Lolly were there.

The time is 09:33am.

Chapter 14

I was glad to find them. We begin to search for Tillie and Dixie but they find us. I do a search and find I have a card showing different objects which people fear the most. Five choices are there and we all peered at it. We think it's the first one that is clowns at a circus. It turns green meaning correct.

Next there is insects, blood, dolls, and ghost. I think the last one is blood and put it as the fifth; it turns green. Richard thinks insects should be third and I say nothing. I trust him. It turns green, which only leaves dolls and ghosts. All agree that ghosts should be at second and fourth should be dolls.

Both turn green and it reveals a number 1, 9, 8, 4. It makes no sense. I throw my mind back and remember Tillie saying she heard something on the machine. She nods and places the headphones on. I hear voices plus music. My friends come round and listen. We have to work together; we know it's true.

I hand the headphones back and Tillie puts them on as it keeps her calm. It is the same for me with the fruit stick. Something in the walls shake. I run to the lift but before we get there, Richard is swept off his feet. Lolly vanishes, Dixie gets pulled through the wall and Tillie gets tackled and falls through the carpet. I stand watching this happen. The lift opens and I step inside. The doors close and it goes down. The doors open and I step out into the car park in broad daylight. It is 10:00am.

In London at 10:10am, Washington and I arrive back at the News Article. We park the car and both get out as it transforms back into his meteor ball. It glows which means it's recharging; half hour for it to finish. The guard at the doors of the building stops us from entering the premises and says, "You and him are fired. Also no more investigating on the mystery. It's coming from Gwen as she has banned you."

I look up to see the office and go to the phone box. Washington follows me. I need money and the ball turns into a coin which surprises us both. I put it in and a screen opens. I press travel, then the office. Washington says "This is going to work." Once I press the button, the coin comes out normally but now it doesn't. This was a different kind of coin.

I flip it over and read the extra objects and the coin changes back into the ball. I watch the guard as the phone box is breaking down into a gate on the floor. The guard moves towards us. I whisper, "Finish it," and it does. A light under my feet glows and I fall quickly, pulling Washington's sleeve. He sees me and moves, and we both leave the entrance.

I fall onto a desk and roll over onto the soft carpet. Washington falls on the desk knocking a cup. He gets up and looks at me awestruck trying to process. I point to the pictures of her doing things—tennis, rugby, judo, running. The last one is a picture of her opening the building in 2021.

We both look for information and he finds a notebook filled with information about meetings as today's date is Halloween Night. First is a meeting with the buyers making a deal; next to it is a paper with names of all fired employees and I spot my and his name. It has a bounty of 1000 pounds each, dead or alive.

He points behind me and I turn to see guards outside. I hide behind one of the computers. After that, he waves to me and I crouch while marching to him. He shows me the invitation to the Gala Party and underneath it, the message reads, 'Join together for ghost of dead and the humans.' Right now, in front of me, Gwen is building something and it will not be the Care Home.

I look at the watch and it reads 10:23am. "Time to find the book and send it to the Home. You have one and there are two right." He nods. "That means someone else has it. On the desk is the girl's name called Isabella Bop. She has my job as a journalist because I am fired." It also has a phone number. I phone it and rings but goes to voicemail which says, "Tonight is the party."

I walk around thinking what to do. Washington stands next to the computer and presses a key to launch into action. It loads but it needs a password. On the sticky note was the password to log in, so he punches in the numbers and letters, and the screen changes. It is the set-up of the party where everyone is going to sit.

It also shows a blue gateway at the centre stage where she will open a gateway. One is built already; so, half of the job is done once she finds the instructions for the portal. One is in the Care Home with Hannah and the other is somewhere here in London.

The guard is at the door. Washington and I were ready. We swing open the door which takes the guard by surprise. He turns but I punch him in the face, breaking his visor. He stumbles backwards and I kick him in the shin. I grab his shirt and lift him to my face and laugh at him.

I let go and we walk past him. Washington opens the book and the first page is the Home with all the heroes moving around. He is about to turn the next page as the lift doors ping open but on the side, two guards come out with guns. They fire out bullets at me. It is time to show them how good we are. I take the silver ball and spin it around and the bullets stop.

Each one moves backwards. The machine clicks, about to fire. I tell Washington to go. He runs like a raging bull and takes both guards and the guns. I stop spinning the ball and the bullets fall next. Washington turns the page and it is the portal that Gwen is going to use at the party. In eleven hours, we have to find *Pop Sweet* and the instructions.

Chapter 15

We get to the entrance and it is Gwen with the police force. It is time to get that book. She wants to talk. Gwen walks up to us. "You can't stop me. The ghost will destroy both worlds, it is power greed. Also, my name will be in the papers." She laughs and takes the guard's gun. She clicks it.

I at the same time shake the ball and it disappears into my body. She fires at me and hands back the gun to the guard and tells them to follow her. Inside, my stomach feels funny as the bullet went right though it and left no mark. I breath in relief as the skin closes around the hole. I click my fingers and the guns come flying.

The guards spin around. Washington smiles and joins in as well. By accident, I poke myself in the eye and it comes out on my fingers. I point it at them and it grows in size, making a shield. I click my fingers and the guns stop moving. Washington and I push forward to the exit. Once out, we head straight to the Underground Piccadilly Circus Station while I poke my eye again to put it back in the socket. We head for the train.

It is 11:00am. I'm standing in the car park of the Home. This is crazy. They were in front of me and now gone in seconds. I walk up to the entrance door. The ground underneath starts falling and I watch as all the stones fall until it reaches the barrier. I have to find the rest as time is flying fast. Some light shoots into the sky and the barrier is breaking slowly. It's not long until the destruction of the Home.

Chapter 16

I watch and head to the main entrance as a whiz of wind blows in my ears. The ghost is there normally in the dark but it was desperate for something. I pull the Fruit Stick and press the blue button and see the wooden rail. I move the stick right at the ghost and it looks at me. I press the blue button and it spins the circle to the yellow button which has a list of objects like balls, discus, axe, guns and laser.

I select the ball option and lots of balls come up. I press the first one and it is an orange and yellow ball. I flattened it out as a frisbee and threw it. In four seconds, it transforms into a ball but the ghost catches it. It squeezes it so hard that the puff is gone. I press the button for a ball.

A green ball gets thrown and it explodes in its face. I press the yellow button which came back to the menu and press it again, it is the stick with all colours. The spirit grabs me and sends me through the glass door. I land in the main hall and the glass door floats back into place.

My back hits a chair like I just happen to sit there. The ghost sneers at me. The small button in the middle clicks and makes a beeping sound. It's trying to send a signal to someone beyond the Home.

It is 11:15am in London Piccadilly Circus. Washington and I are waiting and the ball beeps. He grabs and spins it as he answers, "Hi, Washington here."

There's no answer but we hear a voice, "Think you can stop me, Hannah. Well, the ghosts are ready and we stole the gems and the instructions for the portal. So, good luck. Try Julie Kid Long again and she will kill you. Stay down, worthless person. You think you are the only person that matters, push them away to the side."

I retort, "That is a cranking lie to my mind."

The last words we hear are, "I took your friends Richard, Lolly, and Tillie plus Dixie in the home somewhere. Also when I did this, I took the gems and the instructions for the portal. It is built already." The ghost is gone as Washington and I listen. It was Hannah. The ghost has already built the portal and has the gems. It only needs Gwen to build the other half at the party and the world we know will become a disaster.

I look around and make it through the turnstile and into the station. A bullet hits the metal machine and I stumble to the side. Washington reads the map to see which way to go. We want to go South Bound towards South Kensington where The Nation Party is.

We turn to see Gwen and some others next to her, all looking at us as she reloads a bullet in the chamber. She yells, "Stop, Washington. You two are not getting on the train." I samba shake and Washington has the meteor ball ready. The silver light travels down the arm into the fingers as the ball is formed.

The lady in a dress, the girl with teeth, magic, mind moving powers, a girl with the acid like skin and the boy who looks guilty in my mind reappear. I really want to strangle him but I smell something…

Bang! Quinn pushes Gwen and the bullet smashes the light above our heads. Quinn yells and he comes towards us and shoves us to the escalator while I have the silver ball and Washington holds the book. We run down the escalator and Lauren fires a red circle that slices the ceiling and we head down as the little wall comes apart.

Following us, the lady with acid spits something long and stretchy. The young girl in the dress lifts the steps of the escalator we were going up on. Quinn shoots a beam at the girl and she stops; the steps fall down. We make it to the bottom. Gwen is right behind them and fires at the wall and breaks a sign above our heads. Quinn closes his eyes and makes a black ball like a bubble. It expands as they approach.

Janet circles her hand and a gate appears behind him. He laughs, then nods and jumps through it. I press the ball and make an invisible shield. They can't see us but the action is happening. All of them go after Quinn and he leads them away. We run for the train. I forget that when I don't press the ball, the shield is not active.

Gwen sees us and sprints for the station. I get on the train and smile, sticking my tongue out at her as I pass her leaving the stop.

Chapter 17

Once at the stop we need, Washington can hear the girl's voice. It is Hannah in the Home but how can we speak to her through something and fast as we don't have long. The time is 11:30am. We step off the train and see a ghost. Washington can see it too but it makes no sense. It says, "You made contact with Hannah; as she can see me, any friend can see as well."

It clicks its finger and the tracks rise up onto the platform and the wires from inside the ceiling fall down onto the tracks. They make sparks and the sound of a horn is heard. A train is coming but the ghost is gone. In the tunnel, the train is coming fast. Washington opens the book and turns two pages but there's nothing. It is still the instructions.

Suddenly, the tracks flatten straight and the wires slot back in the wall and the tiles move, building a wall at the entrance of the tunnel. We hear the screeching sound of the train as it is slowing down. It gets slow enough that the wall breaks and tiles fly everywhere.

She stops them. I see the train arrive at the station to a complete stop. I turn to see a girl holding a book, the one we are after. It is now or never. We go after her down a long tunnel with bright white light in the wall all along. She is fast but we nearly catch up. She opens the book and mutters, "Floor rise," and spikes pop out from the ground.

Washington throws the ball at the wall and there is a hole. We jump through it and come out landing a few feet behind her. We are just arms-length from the girl as a spike shoots right in front of me, almost slicing me clean. Holding the silver ball, I spin it around and the girl moves backwards a few steps. The last of the spikes come down and I stop it; time catches up and we reach the girl.

Washington picks up the meteor ball as he runs and makes it. I stand looking at the book. The girl shakes my touch and closes the book, asking what we want. I put my hands up in the air. "We need the book and off you go." She stares at me. Then another woman passes by with curly black hair, short, slim, strong core, lovely personality, wearing a T-shirt and hoodie over the shirt, long jeans, and white trainers.

She looks at me and eyes the silver ball. I hide it in my pocket and she smiles and waves. As my mind is focusing on the girl, Washington catches up to see the girl leaving the station.

We wait looking at the girl. Her next words are that how did we know about her. "Gwen's office had the number and the invitation to this party," I answer. Isabella shrugs her shoulders. We explain briefly about the danger with our friends in the Care Home and we need the book to help stop this ghost.

Minutes later, the lady with the nice clothes comes back "Heard about the gem," she interrupts. I look at her quickly and think. "Oh, by the way, where are my manners. My name is Sunshine." We both shoot a glance at her. These few words make me feel off balance. "I am here for the gem that Gwen has."

I wave to her to come down the stairs. Both listen when I say, "I need the book for the Home and you get the gem tonight at the party." Both have quizzical looks but I breath in relief when the girl in the hoodie says she is fine with that.

The other one says, "I give the book only if you get me the story of the night." Washington and I think about it. This will get us the book and also, we can crash the party, so the answer is yes. She hands us the book and stays with us until the party. She nods and tells that she also needs help with information. We head out to the streets of South Kensington.

At 12:30pm, I am standing at the main entrance looking for the others. She says, "Don't try or she will kill all of us." We walk down past the Dine Area which is open normally. The door is closed and I step forward and see the bones of a human. A musculoskeletal sits and drinks water, and it passes through the system. We watch it go to the stomach, down the liver into the bladder, showing how the human digestive system works.

My foot steps on a floorboard and it creaks. The skeleton turns from his seat and looks straight at me. I stand up and throw the chair. Its back stretch and in the shoulder blades are the muscles. I saw nothing in there, because the muscles are wrapped around the ankle – the tenders were along the door frame. I move back. Hands holding the wall pulling on the muscles…it was free—the body gone.

I look up and right in front of me, it rips one of the bronchi bones and jolts forward. The bony fingers are inches away and I fall backwards and scramble into the Nurse's medication door. This time it was close. The teeth click like a lighter about to ignite but the backbone shakes the head. I turn right and crawl, then getting to my feet, I run for the lift. It stands there and turns the head 360 degrees, like some exorcist demon.

I jog past the nurses' office and look inside. I see a big ugly scaley fish, like a piranha, biting something. Blood splashes on the cabinet on the right and laptops on the left. I continue to move and feel a touch of a green plant on my shoulder. I look up to the ceiling and there is a vine.

Then another bit whips fast at me but I duck under and run deeper into the hallway. There are no lights. I have the Fruit Stick so I grab it from the pocket and make a light. I see the tea trolley but it has been gone since this morning, a trick in the Home maybe. I get closer and see there's nothing on the top. A metal frame moves to the middle.

There's a bit of blood and eyes are floating inside it. I'm about to stand up but on the top, there are stinging nettles along the surface. I move my hand away fast and then a vine from the door frame of the Tea Room lashes at me out of nowhere. It misses and hits the button for the lift.

Then the kitchen door flings open as something grabs the corner. A hand and it is blue. The ghost is trying to scare me. It is quick and it changes into black ink. It extends to the roof of the frame and both sides form a spider web. In the middle is a ball that shrinks and then splits apart…

…nothing.

A radio comes flying right at me. I dodge it and as the lift doors open, it goes right inside. I put the Fruit Stick in my pocket and jump through into nothingness as the interior has no buttons.

Chapter 18

Next thing, I am swimming. I see the inside of the lift is an aquarium. I see all sea creatures from the sea: fish, white-tipped reef sharks and turtles, manta rays, crabs on the bottom, jellyfish, squid, eels, and starfish swimming around. I'm exposed to anything though. If something touches me, it could damage my body or kill me possibly.

Fascinated, my eyes spot the ink as it seeps into the water and floats up. It is scary. I just think about my friends now. I swim upwards and turtles swim just behind. Then it is a shark with its teeth about to bite me but misses me. I swim to the door and the turtle flipper skims in the middle. I lay straight in the middle and head for the door again.

The shark is whisking past and on the bottom is a Reef Tipped Shark along the sand. It is an amazing sight to see. My eyes are bouncing all over the place. I see an eel pass by. I get to the door and press against it. It wobbles like jelly which was not a good sign. Breathing is important. I see a turtle; it's not bad. The shark is here again.

I breathe. It bites a fish. Just at the tip of my toes the turtle turns around with its eyes dark as the night; on the side climbs a Flamingo Tongue Snail. It moves right in front of me and my hand is inches away from this creature. I push harder at the wall and my hand goes through, letting the bubbles escape. My arm starts to go inside but my legs are beginning to ache, yet I keep going.

Time is of essence. The burn in my shoulder increases as I press it to the door. It begins to sink though but a shark is right there. Another fish is next to my waist and it opens the jaws. My legs tread water and I move away from the fish. My legs sink through and I relax. The other half sinks through and a shark jolts forward to the fish.

I make it but breathing is not easy. I see bubbles going upwards which means it is nearly at the end. My lungs are burning but I swim at a good pace. It looks like a sewer; empty with nothing but me. I see which direction to head or another gateway made of water. I swim away from the flamingo Tongue Snail.

The black ink is following me and it sinks through. The black ink sticks to the floor and crawls along. It changes to spots all the way up. The more it comes in, the more the picture gets clear. It is an octopus few strokes from the opening of the water-mirror, in the same tunnel. I see Richard and Lolly which gives me hope.

I turn on my back and use my arms as flippers. The Flamingo Tongue Snail had my big toe and it hisses absorbing the skin. I feel like burning but I push once more and let go. Next, the tentacle is about to reach my ankle and I feel the holes over my skin. One more big push and my head enters the doorway. I can breathe again which feels great.

I grab the frame and pull myself out of the lift. Once the legs flop out of the gate, the Flamingo Tongue Snail gets fried as it comes through. I'm happy to see my friends and I sit there freezing cold, staring at them.

The Fruit Stick is safe and it makes a noise. I answer it like a phone, "Hello," in a soft voice. "Hannah, we are sending you a book to save the gate before the party." Then the signal breaks up. I look up to see Richard and Lolly out of breath. They point and I see a wasp flying in the halls. Tillie is one floor down and Dixie is in the Wing.

Something is on each floor, for example, on the Top Floor I find myself that the home is moving frequently because the time is now 13:30pm. I get up and go to the stairs leading to the Middle Floor. I shout down and hear a voice; it is Paige's. She yells and a red beam is fired at the carpet. It moves upwards blocking the creature. I call her name and say let's go. She runs up the stairs and watches the vines.

I get my Fruit Stick out but not quickly enough. Richard touches the white door and his body changes colour. He makes the handle bars on the wall point to the thing. Paige sees as a vine slashes at her. She jumps and hangs onto the bar and moves along to the next and so forth. She makes it to the floor with us.

The creature is not there and the vines still there slide up the wall, slithering along the floor to the Wing. I ask where is Dixie then I see her with Tillie. Tillie has the machine with the headphones, allowing her to see windows getting smashed and glass everywhere. As the four of us reach the Wing, we feel something black is behind us.

A boy falls and rolls. He closes the hole and it is gone and opened in Eastleigh. The villains are not there but him. Richard and the others are ready to fire. I stop them and turn to see us. "Hold the fire," and waves his hands to save some time "The others want to destroy you guys for the portal, sent them away from here; plus, I have powers. I am not evil; just want to use them for good use but instead need help from you."

He whistles and a black dart flies in our direction, hitting the vine that had crawled in through the broken window. My friends and I are in surprise. Richard says, "Do something and I will hunt you down."

"No threats please," I say to Richard and apologise. He is just not happy to see someone else end infront of them. "Okay, I want to kill the ghost if you teach me." We all nod and head to the Wing to prevent the reign of the ghost and stop history from repeating itself.

Chapter 19

It is 14:00pm. at South Kensington Station. Walking on the streets we see the French Embassy. The girl with the book wants us to help with a story. The other one is hoping to find the gem. Along the street, there is a boy in a car. He pulls to a halt, winds the window down, and says, "Get out of here, Washington and Rose, go. The police know about the incident on the cruise and blame you. You have a bounty of lots of money for capture."

He winds the window up and drives away fast, leaving us to find shelter. Nowhere is safe, I think. Sunshine is quick and makes a call to her friend, D-Man. He says to head to the Lyceum Theatre. A few clicks and he manages to open a line from the bench. Right round the corner is a police car, so we run across the road and sit on the bench. I go first with Isabella, next are Washington and Sunshine with the phone.

She thanks her friend, D-Man. He moves a chair. "Are you doing the early dance?" She stops and goes quiet.

"No," the answer came with a little laugh. We make it to the thing. "I will be at the entrance to greet you," D-Man says and Sunshine hangs up. The door is a revolving one. Washington, Isabella then me, and Sunshine make sure the police are not following. We step onto the hard-tiled floor. The inside of the building has spiral stairs. She says to go up.

We walk five floors and she opens the mailbox and her friend is here on time, 14:30pm. Tall, tracksuit bottoms, black shoes, funny and has a dark skin tone which suits him. He wears a bandanna to cover his hair but takes it off. He has dreadlocks and it is a good style for him. He slaps our hands each, even Sunshine's.

The stairs are not like any staircase; it's clear glass and we can see underneath. As he turns and lifts his leg, a puffing noise comes from the rear end, and he laughs. Washington, Isabella, and I are surprised and we burst out laughing. Then we begin the climb to the fifth floor.

Once at the door, the floor scans her feet and a voice comes out and says, "Welcome, Sunshine and D-man, and friends," which means us.

I ask "That's right?"

Sunshine giggles and scan her eye at the door. It buzzes open and we all go in and it closes. We explain to them why we need the book. "I am after the gem and want to save the Home. D-Man is a high computer tech and he also plays video games, looks at stuff on social media and so far, as he said, the news wants you two because of the cruise, which is not your fault."

He waves his hands and points to the screen. We all wander over to the camera system. Gwen is giving instructions to build a gate. "Once that is done, one person has to go in and stop the gems from the middle, connect both gates and blow it up."

Isabella says, "You can call me Izzy." All of us nod. Washington opens the book and sees dots in the Care Home.

He flips the page to show the instructions for the portal and also the one that Izzy has. He reads the words. Sunshine whisks her wrists and thinks of the Care Home. She pushes the book through and it is gone.

D-Man is excited to have friends to help. It is important to talk about the party and what clothes to wear. "It's all laid out," he says and slides a door open. There's a dress for Sunshine and Izzy. Washington and I laugh because he has to put a penguin suit on for a fancy night.

As we get dressed, there are two costumes there. D-Man says, "We need to find these two people at the train station in London have a direct travel to the station."

All are up for it. Izzy wants to stay with him as she trusts him. He is a good man. Izzy promises not to leave and they will sit at the system. The rest of us walk through the door and the station appears on the ground floor, right in the middle. There's a café to the right and shops on the left. We search to find them and spot the two ordering food in a café named Hunt Lake.

We waltz in and sit down. Sunshine speaks first and both look up. The boy remembers me and Washington from the news. We tell them to shush gesturing with my finger. "Help me beat Gwen." The boy shakes his head and tells his mother. She gasps. He drinks his fruit juice and his mother turns to us.

"You are wanted for a lot of money. My son tells me you need to beat Gwen." All three of us nod in unison and place our hands on the table. Sunshine shows the invite to her. She opens it and reads it twice. "I have been invited to Gwen's party. Come and join because she walks with me in the park as good friends. Thought it would be nice."

"That is why we need your help to stop her. We can only get in with you and begin there."

"Yes, I will go." Sunshine tells her clothes are ready and she has paid for her drinks. We are good to go and it is 15:00pm. We walk her back to the theatre without the police finding us.

Chapter 20

I make it to the theatre and walk in through the door. We make it back to the room to see D-Man and Izzy playing a football game on the PlayStation. He is leading 3-1. Izzy is enjoying herself. She scores and spins in the chair with her hands in the air, shouting, "Come on, no way." The game ends and she loses by one goal. She places the controller on the table and sees us.

We stand there with two new people so introductions are made to Kylie and Eddie Summer. D-Man hands me spring two. In fact places them which indicates a cracking sound. We hear them talking away and scream her name and the sound travels.

In the Care Home, Tillie hears her name and calls me over while I duck through the vines and chop them into quarters to reach them. All are gone as the building turns behind me and the hallway is falling but the pieces are vanishing from here every time. This maybe means the ghost is closer to her revenge than expected.

Charlette is there next to us all and we see her. She points to Tillie with the machine "We can help, get Tillie," she whispers our names through the machine we can hear underneath." That is useful information.

"No need to help. It is all under control relax until the party." But it is was no time stop when so close to the party. Quinn has an idea and the time is 15:30pm in the afternoon. Quinn leads us outside with a table in the Smoking Area and the Activity Arena behind us. We sit in the chairs provided and watch as the world goes by.

It was kind of nice as he told us that he sent the rest of them to another town in the UK. They all sit down before I do. He tells me something in the locker and clicks his fingers and Ding! I hear in the Adult Room.

I walk to the door and go inside this complicated Home. I get to the locker and the key is turning all by itself. I step away and it finishes turning. It flings and a right eyeball shoots out. It misses me and bounces onto the table. I put my hands in the locker and find a pack of cards UNO and Dobble card game.

That's not weird at all that these have turned up in my locker. Along with them is a book. I take the lot back outside and show everyone the objects in my locker. All lean forward to see me open the cards. I deal seven to Quinn. Lolly and Paige ask for the rules and Quinn explains them.

Tillie sits in silence, listening to music. I pull out the Fruit Stick and press the green button. I scan the deck chair and do a duplicate and put it away in front of a lower table. I place the Dobble pack and give one to Tillie. She sees the card, takes the headphones off and tries talking through her smile.

"Count to three—One, two, and three name the first thing on the card." I take the card and find the next one and I see the others playing theirs.

It is 16:00pm, and I lose to Tillie, but she speaks about the gems and about them being in line. Her machine needs to put in another mix tape. She reaches in her pockets and one is there but we are receiving things randomly. All hear Charlette saying, "We want to help you but we trust you, so I gave the tape." She smiles towards the underground Care Home and checks things.

Tillie presses open and slots the tape in. The tape rolls round and is all set, ready for later. She says to me, "The gems are making a source of light for the homes to join and I was afraid to tell you that the gate is at Nation Party in London." We all are surprised and we laugh.

A snigger comes from Quinn but then gets serious. "We shouldn't be afraid. It feels nice to share stuff that will help the mystery." Tillie goes red and moves to the other table. Paige swaps places with me and now she plays Dobble and I watch UNO. This time around seven cards are dealt to me. I oblige to join in and it is fun. We can no more waste time today. We need to think about the clues for the mystery but I want to enjoy it with my friends around me.

On the two springs, I can hear them playing card games and Tillie mentions the power source which can help us, but how. It is time and other than waiting, there's nothing we can do. We have all the clues. Washington and I study the book with the dots and as we turn the page, Eddy sees the images of something. It clicks.

D-Man and he both think fast and answer, "It is Lego pieces." All of us stare at them.

D-Man mentions again, "It is Lego pieces in order to build this gate, she'll use the street outside and change it into Lego but she needs a full moon, which is tonight."

All say together, "Halloween Night?" He nods. She is going to use the moon to harness the Lego. It was time to end this. Sunshine tells us how she knows about all this. She was on the cruise and in London with us a few hours ago. Also, the building is different not the same.

Sunshine smiles. "I am from the year 2040, four years from now, and I had a watch. I didn't steal it. Also, I had the gem but then it was gone. I had to find the watch but it glitched and sent me back four years to this year 2036. That is why you saw me on the ship and in the station at Piccadilly."

All of us accept it and D-Man follows up with that they didn't want to scare us. The day has been full of little information. My head is fine. There is not much happening so it is cool. We all get up to dance. D-Man and Sunshine laugh and he puts music on the computer We all dance in the space provided, enjoying the night.

Then I hear a crash in some hallway through the springs on my fingers, which means something is happening at the Care Home. I listen to what is going on as the dots move around. I see something happen and the book changes colour as another six dots show on the page. I go to touch it and it expands into the entire home, allowing me to look at all the floors.

All stop to see as the home glows in my hands. I spin to see things on the floor. Through the springs sound of crashing and breaking can be heard.

Hannah is in trouble I think. She needs help back in the Care Home. Hannah and her friends are playing cards and come to a stop when the floor starts shaking. The gate which is pad-locked rattles and flowers blowing in the wind, then stop. Light comes from the Activity Arena. Paige stands up ready to fire. Next, we all stand up.

Lolly with her eyes closed watches as a Prime Frost walks downstairs in a station. She immediately knows which station it is. Daisy is next to her and tells about how the theme park is opening soon. We need to hunt this girl. They waltz into the café in St Pancras International Station and the vision stops.

Chapter 21

It is 17:10pm and we all look at Lolly who sits down saying it's hard to control these things. The rest of us didn't mind. Now it tells us that multiple people are after different objects that we have no idea about. Suddenly, a scream echoes in the house breaking the cold silence. I turn to see a person in the window in front of us. It laughs. It is that ghost who stands there, watching.

It is freaky. It clicks its fingers and is gone for the time being. We all wait as the house turns at the front. We all watch as the brick wall shifts out and the Top Floor at the middle moves as a ferris wheel to the bottom; the Bottom Floor is now in the middle and Middle Floor is at the top.

It is 17:30pm. I move past the fire exit door which leads into the building. I get closer to the window to see inside. A doll that spits acid stands there. I jump back. It walks forward and the doll becomes a teenager. It spins round playing with its hair in a ponytail, its skirt is knee length, has long legs and a strong core, and her teeth are so white that they gleam in the Home.

I cough and it looks at me. It spits and the door melts. I step backwards and trip over a wire, falling on my bottom. There is a table made of snakes and they scatter across the floor, slithering away. I stand up and the doll is there. Next to it is its hand which has a broken bone showing in the light.

A hand places on my shoulder and everything goes back. I see Quinn, Richard, Lolly, Paige, Tillie, Dixie, and I was the last one. I point to the building and they see the door is closed. This is the ghost playing tricks.

I get up and stay with them. We all go inside the building to get warm. Once inside, the lights are working in certain parts but then something blows the fuse and the box is in the attic that is above us. Taking the Fruit Stick, I press the yellow button. Then I press again to select a ladder as the thing is up there. Quinn climbs up and uses his fingers to fire at the lock. It snaps and chains broke off.

As we open the doors, it swing outwards and we feel this is the entrance to the attic. I send all of them one by one and then begin to climb up. Something black shoots past into hallway, leading to the other floors. I continue as Paige gives me her hand and helps me up the last few steps.

Tension builds as we get there. It is musty, stinks of dust, and moisture has made the walls so damp. I walk along to see the others. Quinn, then Richard, stop. Lolly didn't make it to him as something stops her; then Dixie. Paige is next. I make it to her but I bang into a wall or mirror. The doors close. This is not happening.

Quinn bangs on the thing and Richard kicks it. Everyone is trapped. The doors underneath my feet slam shut and a wasp is on the ceiling. There's enough space that I can breathe. I put my hand on the mirror and she does the same. It breaks and now me and her let go but the mirror gets back in place. The thing flaps its wings, humming, and crawls down the mirror. I see Paige touching the sides, searching for a way out.

Next, there is a box that asks her what she is scared of. "You will see." I watch as the box opens and a snake slides over the edge. It forms a human shape but is made from snakes. It hisses at her. The wasp is on the floor and see the stinger. It moves the butt with the sharp needle. It's time to do it.

I dive under the slide head first, turning underneath and watching the sting. It rises up as I place my hand on the mirror. Paige does that too and is gone. Next minutes were fast. The sting comes down as Paige pulls me away into her box.

I stand up as this snake thing moves closer. She yells at it and I yell too. The creature moves away and we make our way to the mirror. We need Tillie to put her hand on the glass. She does something and fires, making us move away. I turn to see the thing is now a yellow snake. Paige shakes her head and breathes deeply.

The snake is two metres in size and it moves along the wall. I see another one coming to join the first one. Now there are two snakes. I do not like snakes. I try to breath and walk towards the mirror and Tillie moves towards us. She places her hand and it is gone. I now make it to the third box. The trick is to place hands on the glass and join together to get out.

Quinn is frozen in the spot and sees something but we are too far away. Tillie points to a little bug in the corner—a brown hard shell and lots of them crawling. They are cockroaches. Then they are on the ceiling. One of these things falls right in front of us. It whispers to the others with its antenna, telling them to do something.

We move to the mirror but the cockroaches burst into slime. As the shell breaks, they grow in size every time. Now we have two giant things here. We place our hands and Lolly does too. It falls and all three of us jump out of the way. In her space, there is plenty of room for us. The next thing we do is wait and shush us.

All four of us stand in silence as we watch the dark space in front. Something moves and jumps forwards. It was green, had dark black spots and it is standing in silence. It croaks which makes my heart beat hard; Lolly moves to the right and we follow. The toad jumps and it makes the sound again. In the distance, moves another toad, at least five come inside the room and they jump.

We place our hands on the mirror, Richard puts his and the glass vanishes. Tillie sneezes and the toads jump right at us, their long legs closing the gap. Paige goes first, Lolly, Tillie, and then me. As the toad sticks its tongue out, I step in time and it sticks to the glass. Richard joins now and we approach Quinn.

In this one, it is very quiet; silent as the night. We approach. The time is 18:15pm. A set of house keys hit the floor in front of all five. Paige moves as something in the shadows moves with her. She takes the keys and throws them into the darkness. We all move forward to Paige and the keys come flying back. We all jump to the side and I go right with Paige and on left Richard, Lolly and Tillie go.

The creature's hand comes into the light as the keys were tossed. It is a scaley reptilian. It claws the floor and leaves marks. The skin has bumps all over the surface. It goes back into the dark shadows and the lights turn off. The room goes dark and a hissing sound comes. The creature is moving and it jumps. Paige whistles and a red light glows in the dark room. We both turn and see the creature's whole body and the long tongue licked me. Tillie, Richard, and Lolly come towards us and the creature is there. It roars and pounces on the prey. We all touch the glass waiting. Nothing…

…Whoosh! We all stumble into another room and the glass reappears with the creature slammed into it. I look around to see Dixie in her human form right in front of us. She gestures to us to not move as she joins us. We watch the shadow as it tries to scare each one. The ghost is trying to break the group apart in order to rule the home.

This has a long tongue like the creature in the box before, but this one sticks to the glass. It has a wide body and this creature is moving across nothing. I see footprints on the floor heading for the glass on the left. We all move slowly and Dixie points to the glass. We all should follow her orders if we want to finish this task.

The creature flashes in the light. It is a chameleon using the technique of camouflage. The head turns and the one big eye stares at us. Tillie presses a button and the creature screams. It faces us and spits the tongue which hits the wall. It runs for us and it is now when we push her to the mirror. I nod. Lolly and Richard are there with their hands up ready.

The creature gets to the end but the feet block the path. The body is closing fast. My body squeezes against the glass and it breathes air on me. Then a noise comes from behind and it turns. I hear Dixie yelling as she turns into human form and then invisible.

The creature uses its eye to pinpoint her and fires its tongue, but this time, It has a burning sensation. As it hits the glass, it melts the glass and it breaks apart. Another one opens its mouth and coughs. Dixie changes to human and the tongue launches at her. She grabs the thing and burns her hand for a second then let's go and runs.

We all go up and put our hands together and wait for Quinn to see us. He places his hand and quickly the mirror falls down. The chameleon moves fast and starts to move its tail which has hard skin. It is about to hit and bang on the glass. We make it to the final room.

Chapter 22

Now all seven of us are in the last room together. Quinn looks at the ceiling and moves around the room. All tricks are the basic stuff people normally are afraid of. We look up to the ceiling as three coloured balls fall through. One bounces and explodes, covering the floor in slime.

The second ball is red and it does the same thing; and the third one is orange but inside it has red slime. We all move under to see as the bucket turns and red slime falls onto us. We all are sticky as now all seven are covered in red slime. The floor is half covered with it too. As we stand there, now body parts and things start falling at a quick rate—guts, joints, bones, intestines.

The glass has the ghost who is laughing at us. I move but slip while trying and hit the floor. On the other side, Quinn in his dark coat and clothes is drenched and smells bad. He tries to move but also falls down. We all are slipping and sliding and a dark hand bangs on the glass. It vibrates and the sound comes first, then the movement in the mirror gets closer.

The light is still alight and makes a sound. Richard slips in the middle. I try to grab his hand and manage to do so. Lolly took Dixie's, and they join with Richard. Quinn turns to take mine but I feel something, not a hand but a body part. It's an intestine and it makes me queasy. I manage to find his hand and grab it.

Tillie steps forward but falls face down into the river of slime. She thrashes up for air, shakes to see if we got there, and Paige is right in the middle. She lifts her legs but they get stuck trying to undo the thing. A black hand reaches for the shoulder, turns and fall backwards. I yell to Tillie and she checks for the mix tape.

As she dives forward, I take her hand and the whole room goes back to normal attic. We all sit there breathing heavily, covered in slime.

I get down the ladder then all do and stand there. The time is 19:30pm. We think of the puzzle. Quinn is alive and wants answers. I give him a brief one, "Ghost is tormenting us."

"Thank you," he answers, looking for the shower room, which is on the Middle Floor. We stay together while heading to Middle Floor. I remember the pictures in the hallway later. Now the ghost is going underneath to destroy which means it gives us five seconds before it collides with us. Stan, who was the KP in the kitchen, is eating an apple.

A piece of glass slices his hand and blood erupts. Then he shakes it and blood drips but a new hand starts forming; all the muscles join together and the nerves, then the skin, but it is all white because he is a ghost. "The name is JKL. The name that is never mentioned is ready for the other phantom at 21:00pm."

We thank him and he adds extra information. "Stay as a group. The ghost despises that weakness." We get to the Middle Floor and find the Shower Room. Quinn is first to have one then everyone follows after—Tillie, Paige, Lolly,

Richard, Dixie and lastly me. Once done, we head to the kitchen.

Then, in the corridor, a circle blows. The Care Home is full of surprises. A group of people land there. Quinn mutters under his breath as the leader introduces themselves as Sinister Seven. "Hello, daughter, are you surprised?" She says. I look at her with anger and they start firing lights and magic balls.

Chapter 23

Tillie presses a button on the mix tape player and it plays a song. It is an upbeat, fast-paced song, and keeps up if you can. "We enter the Care Home and left clues to solve a mystery. In two days try and stop. We will go to the party." A white light ring forms around Tillie's waist. She does a hula hoop action and fires at the group.

They move out of the way and Janet moves the panel without touching it by using her mind. Lily throws a ball of magic but Richard gets in the way. It hits him. A young woman behind spins her wrist and red-light pulses towards us. Paige presses her vein and puts her eye on the hole and fires back. I am in the middle of this cross-fire.

Tillie sings a little more, "Come on, try to stop us and fight. Yes, we are the heroes, getting to the party one way or another; putting the puzzle together as it ends tonight. Every minute counts. Playing the tape and helping my friends; if it means hurting you then I will not forget to aim. Yes, we are the heroes."

Again, the light is around her waist and she presses, the light transferring to her hands. She makes a ball and throws it at them. Janet moves, Lily jumps to the side and Lauren misses. It fades out and we run for the entrance.

Back in D-Man's apartment, we can hear everything and also the others as well. I share the rest of the information I caught before cracking again. I lost the signal. I go to join the others. I check his computer and there is a picture of him showing off his muscles in swimming shorts. I read the time; 19:10pm. The time is nearly there already.

Sunshine gets up and points to the room as she shows the clothes. Washington, Izzy, Kylie, Eddy, and I laugh. It's time to get dressed. D-Man is amazingly dressed in a T-shirt and shorts. It is warm in the room and he is ready to guide us.

Once ready, all dresses are stunning. Kylie and Sunshine have a fishtail spilt at the end of their dresses. Kylie's is aquatic blue colour and Sunshine's is red, with silver earrings and also a purse. My dress is dark black. It's a beautiful dress with flower patterns and it's knee length. I spin around and feel nice. Izzy has a gold one, it's the right size, just covers the knees and she puts on high heels.

The bell rings. I see tuxedos and laugh. One is of a bigger size and the other is for Eddy. We leave the room and tell the boys it is their time to change. Both huff and come out seconds later. Kylie smiles and Eddy gives a weak smile. It is time to go. We head for the door but then sirens flash at the bottom. It's the police; how did they find the place?

Sunshine runs to the room and grabs a suit like Washington and Eddy's and thrusts it to D-Man. He looks at her and nods. "You are coming as well or the police are bound to arrest you. Do it, D-Man; there's no time to lose!" He shakes his head and goes into the room. As he is getting changed, we look at Sunshine as she sets a travel gate to the entrance of the Bow Street Royal Opera House.

D-Man is ready and he shows off himself. We clap and he bows as a true gentleman. The gate is ready and we hear footsteps coming up the stairs. We all go through and D-Man says his goodbye to the room and steps into the light. The world changes. The street is all lit up. The Opera House is brilliant at night.

There's a café rouge just on the street opposite of it named 'Messy Place', because it is a mess but full of colour instead. To attract attention, It has music blaring from the speakers and waiters on roller skates listening to Walkman Mix Tape. A car passes by and throws an object, a ball alight, next to the Opera House. We tumble into the door of the café. Washington brushes himself down and I manage to stand.

We head to the Tube at the end but a police car drives down the street. There's no way out. Izzy wants the book out so I give it to her. She begins to read a spell and a taxi-shaped car's colour changes into a seawater colour and the wheels become bouncy. The body gets wide enough and has seats for all of us. The door needs a hand scan.

She summons the thing and puts her hand; it scans, the green light glows and it clicks open. I wave the others in. Washington gets in, then Kylie and Eddy, Sunshine with D-Man, Izzy, and I are last. I close the door and she does the scan once more. A screen illuminates with a path showing the trip. One word is needed for the destination.

Izzy says, "St Pancreas International Train Station." It jolts off, heading towards the station and the car from the Tube begins to move too.

When the car is outside the station, it stops. The police continue. We sit in silence as it goes by quickly. We file out of the car one by one and head for the big sign which shines bright. There's a black car before at the Opera House. The doors open and guys with guns run towards us. We get to the stairs quickly taking two at a time until the bottom.

Washington uses the meteor ball as it beeps. He hears a voice from the Home. There are lots of insults thrown at one another and he can hear them in the Kitchen. He has a signal as they are fighting to get out. We approach the door. Tillie has the ball which means something.

"Hurry to the party. Come on, Janet, or should I say Mother." Those words stabbed my heart like a dagger. We will get there. I turn to see and these people are closing the gap. I turn the ball and it slows time down for them but we continue to run. I find signage to Underground heading South-Bound on Piccadilly Line.

I check all stops and one has Gloucester Road. The guy rolls something and puffs a smoke. Everything comes back to normal. Everyone is walking at normal speed along with us. It is time. Washington is about to throw it but Izzy stops him. She points to the cover of the book and nods.

She reads and the tiles on the floor rise and start hitting the guys. He knocks it and continues. The posters rip from the wall and make a criss-cross line. The guys jump through them but the one behind gets sliced in half. Blood splashes on the wall. We turn at the end and Izzy reads, "The lights fall." The light bulbs shatter and there is glass everywhere.

We run for the train. We get there and in front of us is the list: Pop, 80s song, 50s Rock. Sunshine just leans forward and presses the middle one. She selects 50s songs; it was Ghost hop. It begins to play. "You can talk about the mystery and the accident; keep your head on. We solve the puzzle as October comes round the corner. The home that has friends as they call it the ghost hop." The train pulls into the station but the guys have caught up with them.

It is 19:40pm and we will be there at 20:30pm before the party starts. We all get on the train in suits and dresses. The doors close but two guards make it to the train. It moves along the tracks and the next stations appear on the map on the wall: Euston, Russell Square, Holborn, Convent Garden, Leicester Square, Piccadilly Circus, Green Park, Hyde Park Corner, Knightsbridge, and Gloucester Road.

While that is showing the route, I know which stop we need to get off at. The guys run forward as the train shakes onward, and they fall face down. Sunshine moves in front. As the guy throws his hands, she grabs it and pulls his weight forward, She lifts her leg into his stomach and his knees give away and she slams the arm down on the floor.

I look and she stands on his fingers. The book shakes in my bag. Eddy holds it tight and Kylie moves to touch Sunshine's shoulder. The guard pushes past Kylie and falls on the seats. The other is behind Washington and D-Man and he strikes. D-Man elbows the guard in the face and he stumbles a few steps back. He turns grabs him and throws him into the chairs.

Kylie sits and I watch with Izzy all this. Kylie punches his jaw and it swings back to D-Man. Washington kicks the weapon away, Kylie quickly stretches to grab the pole and swings round her feet, and hits the man in the visor. D-Man helps Kylie onto her feet and we all turn to see Sunshine lift his head and slam it hard on the floor.

Izzy and I sit with Eddy and read what is the next stop as the train jolts forward after stopping at Russell Square.

At Holborn, I feel around in my pocket. The silver ball is in the bag which Eddy has. I search and find it, I feel the ball shaking and the thing goes into my arms. I stand and the guy throws a punch, I didn't see it and it hits the side of my face. I go to the pole and back to my original position where my feet feel like nothing. I laugh as he tries again.

I spin in a circle once and my body swirls more, making a vortex. I grab his shoulder and lift him up. He hits the lights and slams back on the floor. I do it again and then launch him forward to D-Man. He hits like a ball and smashes the window. He falls onto the chair and he cheers Izzy by yelling, "Winner." He feels happy.

I do the samba shake and the light goes to the fingers and then into the ball. I put it back in the bag. The next stop is Convert Garden. Washington throws the gun off the train. The guard feels his jaw and goes to punch her but she moves to the side. Washington stops the fist before it goes and twists it. He bends around and falls, marching forward to him. The train moves again and this stop was Leicester Square.

Izzy and Eddy look at the map and their ears pop underground. Next stop is Piccadilly Circus. Sunshine throws the guard off and the doors close. The light is bright still. Next one is Green Park. We continue as we grab the guard and make him stand against the door. The bag moves and Eddy opens it. He pulls out the book and shows it to us.

Right now, we know the party is close. We need to get there fast. The guard sees it and leans forward. The door opens and D-Man pushes him off the train. The doors close and now we have lost both of them. The map reads Hyde Park Corner. We get there and all of us look at each other breathing in relief.

Eddy smiles and Kylie is sorting the dress. The men sort their ties and look smart in five minutes. The train moves and Knightsbridge is coming seconds later. We reach the final stop of this line which is Gloucester Road. I see everyone is ready to go. We get off the train and head for the exit.

I make it to the exit. Washington drops the ball and walks in; the rest go in as well and I'm the last one. As I did outside the National History Museum in London, I see the bench. Sunshine sits with D-Man and then both are gone. Kylie sits with Eddy and then they were gone. Washington is on his own. Izzy and I sit down and a police car's sirens head in this direction, so we make it fast.

The scene changes. We are in the same place one hour ahead in time to intrude the party and get Izzy her story of the night. The time is 20:30pm.

Chapter 24

It is 20:30pm. I hear silence. It is brilliant for walking around the Home for a place. Then the people find us and the floors start moving and the steps turn. Tillie is on the Middle and she goes to the bottom, Dixie is in the Wing safe for now. Richard and Lolly are on Top and they go to the middle which leaves me going to the Top.

On the Bottom floor, the hall goes dark, nothing is visible. I use the Fruit Stick and a light shines. I see that the carpet has footprints, more like a trail made, but no one was there. Something wet drips from the ceiling. I point the light in front of me and a ghost is standing there. It waves and jumps up and down, and touches the floor laughing.

I breathe in and close my eyes. I open them again and the ghost is not there. Near the door frame two metres, it yells, "BOO!" I startle away and drop the thing. I find it and shine the Fruit Stick again but all is gone. The words echo, "Better stop me, Hannah." It is Sherry's voice. What we have here, I look around.

A box is there but I don't touch it. I lift the lid with the tip of my toe and a ghost statue goes round in circles and a tune plays. It finishes and the lid closes. Something is right in front of me. It is the black creature I have seen before. It roars and

I point the Fruit Stick at it. It backs away but then the mirror smashes, the picture falls of us in front of the Home. But we didn't take that photo.

Suddenly, it melts into a red liquid in my hands. I let go of the picture and the creature swings its hands at me. It hits me in the jaw and I get whacked on the wall. I feel dizzy. It goes again but I duck under and touch the rail to steady myself. The Fruit Stick in my hand points up and it screeches and moves away.

Opening the gate, I place a foot on the stairs and wobble down like I was drunk. I make it and the feeling is gone after a minute. The pole moves off the wall and slips off the stair and goes under it. I see Janet in the front waiting for me to move. I use the Fruit Stick and press the red one and point to the window then move to her. The window rips off the building and shoots right at her.

Janet stops it one metre away from her face. I march forward and press the button, it drops and glass is now all over the floor. She looks at me as I rugby tackle her into the Wing. Janet stays on the ground for a while and the light is glowing. It is Lolly and Richard now, then all of us are there. We open the doors to the Activity Arena and in the middle is a circle of Lego; the gate and gems are outside. A ghost stands before it and says, "Too late." The building starts to shake.

Washington and all of us walk to the entrance of the building which looks stunning and the clouds are moving. It's not long till the full moon and gate is built. Gwen sees us and French kisses Kylie and her son. She glares at me and does the same French kiss to D-Man, Sunshine, Washington, and Izzy. She welcomes us to the Nation Party which starts now. Speeches are at 21:00pm.

Chapter 25

I take in the ambiance walking along a stoned path with flowers engraved into them. There's a water fountain as we get closer to the door. Gwen is so happy but still glares at me. We get inside and Gwen says, "Isabella, it's nice to see you. Report about how this will be the best event of the night." Izzy nods and turns to the people who are coming.

I see there are a lot of people. One I see is a woman in a pink shirt, black jacket, long black trousers, and make-up; the other is in a silver dress that is glistening in the light. She has a black sack on her shoulder talking away. We didn't catch her name because instantly we have another one coming this way in a blue shiny dress.

She has a coat over her shoulders and blue crystal shoes to match the dress. Her eyes are the same colour and as she gets closer, we see her and smile. She looks like someone from a restaurant walking past but has manners. "My name is Lucy White." She heads to the building. The dress has a lovely pattern of flowers.

I quickly think about the woman in the silver dress but didn't get her name. Just after that, we all see a woman pass by wearing a black dress, which allowed her to move her feet, high heels, with make-up, blue and pink hair tied in a bun and a black cardigan. She strides in our direction before coming through. There are two more girls and she gives them a hug as she knows them.

Moments pass and Gwen shakes her hand. This girl has a firm grip and on her wrist, she has a watch with a pink strap and the screen is black. It shines with the moonlight. She is smiley, has a nice attitude, and moves side to side, both pretending to box each other in a friendly way and they laugh. She straightens herself and Gwen says that she is Christine Witty.

Then, the two girls who are friends of that girl that went inside now are here. One is wearing gold trousers and a top with a white bag; the other one is wearing a gold dress which is short, just on the top of the thighs, and showing her legs. Her heels are shining, and they meet Gwen.

I watch the party unfold. It is 20:50pm and I see the clouds move a bit more. The moon is close. Kylie is next to me and asks me if I am good. I stand there as the room is a stunning area. A massive chandelier is hanging from the ceiling, clear glass windows letting light in through from the moon tonight, and a marble floor. There are people dancing. It is a fete. At the end is the gateway that will destroy the Care Home.

I stand in the Activity Arena with my friends seeing the ghost and waiting for something to happen. The light is growing wide and it places the something in the thing fall through nearly there. I move forward and the ghost sees us. I stand up and now all of us know. It giggles and jumps, spreading its arms wide and crossing its feet like dancing.

It spins around in a circle and then faces us. It doesn't move but stops and clicks its finger. The room changes and it is the Café Hunt Lake. There are tables and a counter to the left of me. It sits down with its arms crossed behind the head. I breathe deeply and think that we are in the Care Home. Smirking, Paige sits down but her bottom gets soaked in water as a puddle is on the chair. The ghost laughs.

Next Lolly and Richard sit down but not on the chairs. The candles move towards them and the flame creates a hand and grabs the light, lifting, and the casing smashes, sending fragments in their direction. Then all is gone. Also, Paige's chair is clean but the anger is bubbling in her. It leans into the light and places its hands on the table with a deck of cards of Happy Families.

It deals seven cards to us as one group and itself. "Come play, Hannah and friends." The light swings when it is in line and it stands at the counter ordering a track for music. Time is closing by minutes. I take the cards and we all look. I know how to play. The song plays and we come back to accept the game. Villains roam the Home lose. Our first ask is seven family comics and it says no. "Go Fish."

I pick a card and it is a number from the family, not the one I asked. The ghost says family of action book number three. I look and I have one, five, four. I point to the deck, take one back and continue. The music actually sets us in the mood. I have the stick in my pocket ready to use it but things are smooth. I hear voices.

The party is festive over there. I see the moon pushing through the clouds and shining in the window alighting the room. At the front is something. Gwen moves and I get close taking Kylie with me. Eddy pulls out a computer and starts typing codes to hack the cameras in the building. The girls move as Gwen makes her toast.

Chapter 26

I see something walking through the tables and see Gwen. The girl swings at me and I dodge it. She yells at me; it is the one in gold trousers and has a top that matches the bottoms. She throws a punch but I grab it and take her hair, slam her face on the table in front of me. I hesitate for a minute as I think in that moment.

A person passes with glasses of drinks and I see a flute of Champagne, whip it off the tray and I threw it at her. She covers her head as reflex takes over. She goes to strike but in front of me, there is another glass on the table. I reach it before her hands grasp the glass and she pushes a chair towards me. It makes me move backwards and the table hits my back.

I lean on my stomach pretending to miss something. Above me, I placed my hand on the table and find a glass. I swing it at the girl and it hits her in the face. The table gives me an idea. I push the table away and move around it. She smiles and spins a chair. I step on it and jump over, landing on the chair sitting right in front of her.

I throw a fist sliding out of the chair onto the floor and grab both of her knees and send her crashing into the table behind her. I look around the room to see Kylie with the other one kicking her. I spot a tray and send it as a frisbee to Kylie.

She catches it and swings it so hard at her that it sends the girl into the wall.

Gwen is stamping her feet as a child who is throwing the toys out of the pram. Then quickly her expression changes as the curtain falls in time to reveal to the party the weapon that will destroy both Care Homes in Totland.

I stare, she explained to me I'm such a clever person for not telling her. She did it herself. I grab the instructions and get Izzy to replace me because it will make me rich and popular in the world. "Bravo, Rose, now you know what this is." She spoke it with such sarcasm, it irritated me.

Washington drops the ball and makes the hole. Kylie closes in and Eddy gives me thumbs up that he has hacked into the system and all cameras are down. She lifts the stick and D-Man throws a knife which hits the stick but Gwen deflects it. Sunshine jumps over the table and sidesteps to help. Izzy is watching but has no idea. As she realises, she runs.

I see the moon light the room and the gate change colour. Pieces from the marble flooring rise and shoot right to the gate. Connecting another it changed into Lego pieces, which kept building and when it is done, it opens a blue swirling light going to the Care Home.

Hunt Lake Café in St Pancras International. We are still playing the game as the Home shakes. The light is next to us. The ghost smirks. It is 21:00pm; the thing has started. It asks for action number two which we didn't have. It picks up a card but it is not the one it asked. For our turn, we ask for comic number six. It has it and hands us the card. We make a family and need two more.

The next one we ask is comic number four. It laughs and hands us the right one. We make a second family and win the game. The ghost claps for us. "You played until the gate was opened. You are silly." We gasp. It clicks its fingers and brings us back to the room. The gate is open fully and things start to enter the building.

I see Gwen laughing and walking to the entrance. I stop her and she turns to me. I get to my feet and make it to her. She pokes the stick in my chest, stopping me on the spot. A noise of crashing is heard. Kylie pulls the table cloth and glasses smash on the floor and nods. I look at her and she does it again. Then I hear Izzy saying portal. It makes sense so I run past her into the thing and off I go.

The room is gone and it's all white. A path of clouds lies under my feet. I see everyone fighting to save the thing and on a mission to stop the gate. White light travels above me and it heads to the source I follow that and I can hear voices down the end in the Care Home. It couldn't be.

In the Care Home, Paige's anger is building and a fridge on the side comes right at her. She breathes deeply and we all watch as it passes through her body, then she fires at the glass and makes a duplicate of herself. Next to the drawers, the ghost spins and gets angry. It starts running at her. Richard touches the fridge, which is red silver, and his body changes colour from head to toe.

He is wearing black jeans of the same colour. He whistles and makes a ball and throws it. The ghost is watching the duplicate of Paige and tries to strangle her as the ball is inches away. I look and see the villains are crashing the party at 21:10pm. I get ready and press the red button. Then the TV wobbles off the hinges and I keep pressing, and swing it right to left. The TV rips off the wall in front of them.

Lolly closes her eyes. Richard joins by tapping Paige on the shoulder. She stops firing. As the duplicate fades, the ghost sees us in anger. We leave the room for the Adult Room and catch our breath in the corridor. A red light is shining which means a bad sign. Tillie stands there with the ball which is important, and also with the Walkman listening to the tape.

She pulls out the headphone and speaks to us, "This something for outside for the gate." She shrugs her shoulders. The door moves backwards a little and we see Janet, Daisy, Harley, Lily, and Lauren walk in, ready to attack. I find the door and the light swings but it was too late then. The ghosts are here to rule the world.

Wait a minute. I told myself the light is heading towards us. That turns out to be Kiera, Stan, Charlette, and Mark. They are all here to help us. They made a light reach the door exit, the light is gone…and so the ghost. Charlette shouts, "Julie Kid Long wants us, come on." It leads them away. Quinn is ready to fire darts; Richard gets his hands up; Tillie shows me the ball as if it wasn't for her. Spirit can't argue.

We head to the barrier and the villains fire. They want us to fight so we go and fight. The door opens and all of us step outside. Lighting strikes and water droplets fall. I feel something is happening as more droplets fall, then I hear thunder. The weather has changed; raining here.

All of us stand to defend the Home. It is pouring torrents of rain and lighting still lights the sky every five seconds. It's thunder then light. Harley jumps at us and Richard grabs the girl and while wrestling, throws her over his arm. She pulls his arm and he goes with her flipping over the railing and rolling down to the ground.

I gasp but Tillie needs that ball to go somewhere and she tells us to run. I do and press the green button over the objects like the table next to me. I press again and it grows in size. Next is Daisy who spits acid and it hits the surface, melting it. The others use their power. Lily throws a white ball which makes the plants puff in smoke. Then a blue one on the wall which misses me.

Quinn fires darts at them and jumps over the railing to help Richard. I feel hope as it means it will end well. We continue in the rain to the gate but it is pad-locked. The numbers I tell her are 1-9-8-4, and when she presses each one, a green light appears up in the night. Tillie goes first; next is Dixie, Paige then me and I close it. It makes a thud and click sound, meaning it is locked.

We laugh while running down the long ramp path heading to the gate. Lighting strikes the Home. The roof is spinning. While running, Tillie is in front, Dixie behind, then Paige, and last is me. Near the bottom, a white ball passes me and hits the branch, turning it into ice. I peer over my shoulder and see Lily fire another ball. It hits the rail and they swing, knocking me forward. I lose my footing and fall back.

Paige presses her veins and a hole appears there while running as slowly as possible. Daisy runs along the metal railings and spits. A red light pierces the sky. The fire blinds them and I pull Daisy's hand. It slips off and lands right in front of me. Punching in the face feels good and the sky strikes again. The floors in the home shake up and down.

Things are getting worse. W e have to get Tillie to the gate. Lauren fires a red light slicing the path and makes me go left then right as I dodge it to reach the bottom. Lily produces a green ball, and makes it next to Paige. She puts both hands up, the hole closes on her arm and she fires like she is about to save her.

Instead, she stands there as the ball enters her hands and she stops breathing; this one is a new ability, allowing things in. They yell as it fires back on Lily and her group. We laugh along with Dixie who is there in camouflage. We run to the gate.

I see it as lighting strikes the home. The rooms suck to Activity Arena and the walls tilt left and right. The barrier can be seen in full colour.

Chapter 27

We see it falling down. With every strike, the Home gets worse if I do not go in the thing. Tillie stands right next to the brick wall which is the entrance of the Home. She holds the ball. Janet has the book in her hands. A black beam fires from behind and it flies. I am close. Daisy is moving and I wait to see. Lolly gets there, picks the book up, and throws it.

Dixie, who is in human form, catches it and breathes deeply, making her body invisible. We are laughing when we see it was Quinn who fired. Richard is there with him and both high-five. They face us and I realise that I taught him friends are important. Now is my turn to believe in them. Dixie is in front of me and she gives me the book.

I open the page that has no writing on it. Tillie waves towards the red ball coming from Lauren. That opens the lid of my anger and I give the book to Dixie. I point to the entrance and she runs off. I face them with the Fruit Stick and I finally decide to know what this white button does. I press it and my clothes start to change…

…I am wearing a white wedding dress which has a pocket and it is a shiny white, knee-length dress. There are bracelets on each arm that glow every time they are prodded. I poke at the light and it grows, making me nervous. So, I turn and throw my hands towards Lily and Janet. The bracelets fire a white light right at them, burning the pavement.

Lauren makes a shield to protect herself and the others from the blast. I look at the bracelet and the light is gone. It was like energy—the more I give, the bigger the blast of light. I thought there's hope. I feel boiling anger to see this ghost taking away all things from me, especially the friends that I have made during the two days here. The earrings light up on both sides and I keep going.

I will not let it go that the ghost killed all the ghosts in the Home thirteen years ago. I think of them all that they are here in front of me going 'stop her, kill her', and all are standing with me, trusting us. I hear the words by Charlette, "We trust you, humans and friends." There's one ghost who is nice. They say she is from a theme park.

I let my anger blast from the earrings and Lauren creates a shield to stop it. I step forward and it cracks the shield. The blast breaks her shield and all back away. Janet moves the bins from the wooden gate and I stand there in the rain fighting for the Home. Janet lifts the thing and it is about to crush on Paige but she breathes and drops the thing. Janet laughs, saying, "Come on, daughter, let's fight just you and me."

I shake my wrist in this wedding dress and turn to see Tillie handing something to Dixie and her running towards me. Paige walks out of the dumpster bin patting herself and stops breathing. Her skin is not phasing in and out and she is a normal human again. Anger is building inside her, heating her body. The rain is helping to put it out, but suddenly, the rain stops.

Paige's body goes bright red and she makes knives. She throws one at Daisy but misses her. She creates a duplicate with the reflection of the puddle and it runs to help me have access to the entrance to the building.

I see Dixie and she gives me the machine. Tillie starts to read as the barrier slows down, meaning they kill her to help the gate even more. Richard and Quinn are there. Janet moves them around and lands in front of me. We both get up and are ready to help. I stand in the dress with the mix tape player ready. The time is 21:30pm. It's time to finish the ghost AKA Julie Kid Long.

Chapter 28

First, Lily fires a red ball which hits the floor leaving a scorch mark. Quinn runs firing a laser beam at Lauren but she stops it. Richard touches the tarmac and his skin turns black and solid. He thinks of a bat and in the other hand a ball. He swings the bat and hits the ball and runs. I see Daisy spitting her acid droplets which melt the floor.

Richard's hand is strong and he punches her. She falls. Lauren fires at Quinn but he flicks his wrist and little black darts shoot to distract her. Dixie runs straight and Janet moves the bins from the bottom towards her. When there are inches away only, she stops and jumps onto them. She lands behind then then climbs over again and lands in front of her.

Lily grabs Dixie's throat as her form is still human. Richard taps Lily's shoulder, she turns and a fist hits her head, sending her forward enough to let go of Dixie. She breathes heavily and looks at her the skin which is flashing. She breathes in and out and her arm turns invisible, and then her body. She hits Lily in the stomach and she goes backwards.

Quinn runs towards Lauren and the light around him is increasing in temperature the closer he gets. His body is strong but the pavement is cracking and his body is disappearing. Out of nowhere, a force pushes him to the side.

He rolls out of the way and I pass him before going. I see Lolly in the light and she says to Quinn, "Hannah needs to get to the portal and protect the others, especially Richard."

I see her holding the light and Quinn goes to help her. Lauren fires and the thing slams hard, hitting Lolly in the stomach. She absorbs the thing and dies.

I see Quinn getting furious and he swings both his arms and the black discs shoot from either hand. Lauren's hands are red as the darts slice them. He makes it to her and pushes her She falls on her bottom and she laughs at him. He yells, falling to his knees, and fires a black dart which goes to the side and slams into the floor. Richard joins him and I see them looking at me.

Quinn stands up and fires at Janet and she turns. I have time to make it to the gate so I wave to them. They all clap and Paige turns off her red body as now she is human. While calming down, she still fires at the road and they move close to each other. Tillie is still at the barrier when I leave.

I see the Activity Arena and the gate is sucking in things and the room is going inside it. The Home is breaking apart. Lighting strikes the home and the lights are flashing on and off. The power fuse is gone. The gate is there near the window. I jump up and grab the ledge but the one on the right smashes, glass shatters everywhere.

Janet breaks the window and I hang there with the Fruit stick in my pocket. I swing my legs onto the ledge and pull myself up and enter the room. I see the gate and there is Mia and Sherry. I shuffle my feet and they see me. I stand still and remember the Walkman and the tape needs headphones. I get the Fruit Stick out and press the yellow button.

I'm still wearing the dress and it was a good look on me. I select headphones and put them in the machine. I listen to the music and it is a soft song. I enter the gate and they jump at me but Charlette and Mark divert them. Also, Stan is there who goes straight and I run, following him. I approach the gate and a black creature is at the French doors. It is running as well.

I nearly lose my footing as it closes the gap between us. I see the minutes, drop to the floor and slide into the gate.

Chapter 29

The home is gone and the creature misses me and hits the door. I enter a white hallway and something falls in after me. It is Julie. I have to run which is the intention and I make it a fair bit but she is gone. She didn't follow me. I get to the centre of the gate and see the stones she stole from us. I stand right under it and it is huge.

Then, I hear a voice on the other side of the thing. I ignore it and I stand still as something rises and moves to the middle. It is Julie and she lands on the cloud-filled path. I think I can stop her. She laughs at me. I press the button on the Walkman and it plays a song. I sing along, "Halloween turns things upside down. Halloween is the time of frights and scares and made some friends on the way."

The light starts creating a ring. The more of the song I sing, the more the ring grows. So the music continues as I fire the light but I miss her. It doesn't matter. I'm still singing the next verse, holding the device. "Left us clues and solve the mystery, and hold what is real." The light shoots and it skims the floor, scorching it.

It makes her move again right in the middle of the gate's entrance. Julie jumps as the song reaches the chorus and I sing loud, "Hold what is real so you know what it is to hold what is real." The light gleams as I get ready to stop her. "Friendship is key, that is what I have at the Home." The light fires at Julie's face and she staggers away from me. I look and see that the left side of her face is all black as soot from the chimney.

I place my hand on the gate and realise it is a glass mirror. I sing again, "Friendship is key and you know it is true." The glass starts breaking and I think that if I sing once more, I can break it. Julie swings a fist at me but I duck under it, moving away. Now, the chance is still there, so I stand there ready to fight. The glass keeps cracking.

I see the glass shaking and then smash it. It falls and the gems also fall from the middle. Julie screams and grabs me by my throat. She takes me to the edge as things turn around. "You ruined the celebration of the ghost ruling you humans. Humans wiped out was the goal. It is gone now."

I say to her, "We are the heroes." She brings me back down and punches me in the stomach. As I fall, the headphones fall off too and the Walkman skits to the edge. I see a person. I slowly lift myself to my feet and walk to the headphones and the machine. The ghost reaches for the girl. I put the headphones on but there's nothing.

The mix tape is broken. I get the Fruit Stick out and press a button. I select the green colour and the tape starts rewinding back to before it got destroyed. The girl has a ball and she spins it. Time slows right down but I am still fixing the thing. It plays the chorus and the third verse is starting.

I face the ghost and whistle. Julie turns and the girl keeps spinning. I breathe deeply as get ready to sing. "All clues have been put together, you took everything from me." The light is the bracelet. I nod to the girl and she stops the ball. Time gets back to normal and the ghost comes flying as a rocket. I point the bracelet at it and sing the last words, "Mystery solved. Party ends."

A portal opens just behind the ghost and it whirls. So fast she was going, I see the person moving in trapping it. It continue to sing, *"See what happens on Halloween night;* ending the party once and for all. How far will I go until you don't bother us anymore, saying goodbye, hold what is real." The girl holds the ball and it makes Julie angry.

The light is still pulsing and the gate is still open. "Hold what is real, friendship is key, that is what I have at the Home." I step forward and Julie starts to move but the portal takes her. As she is leaving, she yells and goes into the gate. "Just a little bit of friendship and you know it is true." The portal closes.

I spot the girl and she sees the gems. She picks one up and waves to me. I walk slowly and make it to her. It is Rose. I'm happy to see her. The cloud path behind me breaks and that was back to the home.

Chapter 30

It is 22:07pm and the ghost is gone. I follow Rose fast to the end and we make it as the clouds break. We take one step and then both of us jump into the light. I end up on a hard marble floor in London. There are no tricks from the ghost. I'm in my dress and I look around. Rose hands me the Fruit Stick and tells me it belongs to me.

I thank her and see her group as well as the audience clapping as it is part of the party. Gwen's body is rattling and something black, dark, tall, and scary like thing roars. It smashes through the window and the room goes silent. The gate falls into pieces and the clouds cover the moon. There's no more danger to the world or Home. I panic as I need to get back to the Home. Rose waves to others.

Washington pushes a guest out of the way and makes sure nothing happens. Kylie takes a chair and pushes the girl's shoulder to make her sit and tie her with a cloth tightly; no escape is possible. We wander over to Eddy who shows us the computer with the cameras back online. There's footage of nothing that happened here.

Izzy smiles and she has her story of the night. She thanks me and I look around with my hands in my hair in relief that this is over. Sunshine and D-Man are there too and he grabs a glass of Coke and Malibu (small amount of alcohol). He won't get drunk on it but it was a celebration treat for him in a fancy Penguin suit. He cheers to Hannah and her friends for saving the world.

They all cheer their drinks and in synchronisation, the band of violinists and piano starts playing the intro of 'The March of Figaro Wolfgang Amadeus Mozart'. Washington spins in a waltz circle position and I go with Washington, Sunshine with D-man, Rose and Kylie as good friends. Eddy watches the whole crowd. We began dancing the night away.

At 22:20pm, the girl in the black dress leaves, and just behind her is a woman in a red dress, white cardigan, and high heels who entered before us. She saw what we did to Gwen and she huffs as she follows this girl. A blue light lights up and seconds later, they are gone. I don't know where but not focusing on that now.

I let the night escape away with me hoping that all goes well. Dancing was fun but I have to get back urgently. The others know about it. Washington thinks of the Home as he drops the ball and a gate opens. I couldn't thank them enough and I shake Sunshine's and Kylie's hands and wave to Eddy. I go to shake D-Man's hand but he moves it away as a joke, he then shakes it firmly.

Rose shakes her head and brings me into a hug and lets go. Izzy gives a small wave and I'm off into the light. My feet touch the ground and I see the Activity Arena. I see the destruction of the place and wait but nothing happens. There are no rooms moving or turning upside down. I quickly run to the window that broke before I leave the Home and climb over the edge.

I jump down and run down the ramp all the way to the gate. Once I arrive, I see them on the floor. I spot Tillie on the floor with Quinn. I lift his hand and a gate opens. I shove them one by one into the thing and tell them that it is a prison. Running past them, I wave on the way and I get there. Paige is on the floor and Dixie is next to her. I start checking for a heartbeat but there's nothing.

We all cry. A cough loud enough to get our attention back on her is heard. Tillie sits up. "Heroes save the home." She falls backwards. I utter something between a cry and a laugh. I look and see that all are okay. I close the gate from the inside and it breaks apart.

We hear the last words she says, "Alice Knight will get revenge soon." But that is no worry right now. Tillie is more awake now but still dizzy. We all stand at the entrance.

The Party is not over yet. The ghost comes out of the Underground towards us and allows us to see them playing a song on an electric keyboard. It is a fast intro.

Charlette sings, "Humans come into the home, get trapped in for a long time, things go crazy. Paige has powers that duplicate. Richard can change skin tone and make objects. One is invisible and Tillie has a Mix Tape, and Hannah has a Fruit Stick to stop these ghosts. Clues are there to solve a mystery. Don't believe us but these people are right here. Look at the group of friends, the heroes of the Care Home."

I sigh and see that all are twisting their hips and dancing to it. I copy and the ghost joins in. I look to the stars and enjoy the little things before it's late. The wind blows in the Home which means we have solved the mystery. A green light opens in the road and a man and girl end up here. It is Washington and Rose. They say hi and then they are off. They go back inside the gate.

The End

Aftermath 1

In London, outside the National History Museum, we watch the stars shine in the clouds and the moon is hiding. Suddenly, the moon shines, making the night bright. It is beautiful to see. Then a police car passes by, heading somewhere. We walk down the path heading to Gloucester Road tube, instead, Sunshine takes a phone out and gives us her number to call if danger is around. Also to keep in touch and never be alone.

Washington smiles at D-Man and salutes to him; he does too in return. I laugh and Sunshine shakes hands with everyone before she leaves and heads back to the future. I stand there with tears forming in my eyes. I try not to cry at the end but it runs down my cheek and my heart feels like it is pulling strings. The tears keep coming for a while.

Kylie and Washington are there smiling at me. Is this the feeling when friends leave? Washington drops the ball off and he goes with Rose to France. The rest of us walk and head to Hunt Lake, the café in St Pancras International train station. We sit outside the café as it is closed on the benches. It is cool watching the building late at night when there is no ghost and the party is finished.

I'm in the station with the others and we hear the train arrive at the stop. I'm looking at the tabloid and there's a blue light in the middle. Then, I see a person. It is the girl in the black dress running towards me. She swings her wrist and it is second late. Another woman joins and this one has a red dress.

She is wearing high heels, tall, and wearing a white cardigan. The tabloid has the time 22:52pm written on it. The others and I let this play out. The girl jumps out of the way and the other in the red dress has white hair to the shoulders. She has a good body shape and long legs but she is only 5'4 in height.

She grabs a bin and rolls it towards Christine and says, "Hand the watch and this will end." She sees me and huffs. "Oh, my name is Lucy White…" but she couldn't finish that sentence. The last words of hers were, "Alice Knight will rise on 5 November 2037." She swings her wrist and off she goes.

I remember the girl now. "Christine Witty," I exclaim. She smiles at me. She is the evillest person and this will cause the human existence to end. I process this information as Christine says goodbye to us and whooshes away. She is gone. Hannah and the rest have done well.

We exit the station, heading to a hotel. Then, D-Man holds his device and a light glows for a restaurant in Southampton. We all follow through and make it to the café. We sit in a booth in this place and fall asleep.

In the Cosy Café in the year 2040, a young woman, Sharon Fraise, wearing a dress. It looks elegant and her hair is tied in a French plait. She enters the building and strides to the toilet. She punches a code, it clicks and the toilet drops, opening a door. She walks along a metal walkway down and the pipes shake and rattle. She gets to the end and there are some stairs heading lower under the café.

She scans her face and it opens. There is a slide so she sits down and pushes. Down she goes and comes out of the tunnel onto the meeting room floor. She arrives at the Bureau of Hunters to see a giant clock hanging, telling the time; people heading up and down in lifts to reach their posts and ready for work.

I arrive and someone comes marching to me in a red dress. Her bracelet gleams in the light and has round earrings on. "Sharon." I stand tall to acknowledge her. She hands me a file and taps on it, and I see the pop-ups of information about the situation.

I ask her, "How did they do this?"

She spoke in a hard voice, straight to the point. "They acquired some power from rocks. The blue case ones and the others are red. They were sent to prison." I enter the office and she points to a chair. I tell her that I'm happy to stand. We move along and she points to the screen. A girl and a tall man can be seen and they jump from London 2036 to 2040.

"Her name is Sunshine and her friend is D-Man. They helped this group and the five heroes were on the screen—Hannah and her friends. But hat is not what I am here for. See this." She slides on the screen and a video appears on my screen. It is a girl in London Station that night when Gwen is stopped by a girl in a black dress. She has a watch then she is gone like that. I wait.

"Prime Frost is patient but doesn't want interference with this. There is a theme park on the Isle of Wight in Ventnor and you will help stop this. One thing is for sure there is a team already for you downstairs. I want this sorted because the park is about to threaten the human race and we know it."

Prime Frost is in her black leggings, black top, and her hair is twisted down to her shoulders. There are no further moves. The chair touches the screen again and now we see in the building that there are objects beginning to build in Technology Fun and getting tested. Someone has sent three of these objects to the past, in the year 2036.

I have the debrief and it is time to find the watch and object if possible. My name is Florence Star. A young lady, normal height, has glasses in big round shape. I'm nice to everyone and very smart. I go and meet the team. I get there and see the team. They introduce themselves. "I am Wade Kilo." Next in line is Jessica Violet.

There is a girl who is tall, fair, with brown hair. She looks down as she is shy to talk but still gives me her name. "Freya Ants," she says quietly.

I continue down to another man. "Oscar Hunt, Madame." This one speaks two languages—French and English. The last one is Charlie Sky who speaks a little Italian, Spanish, and English. I have two people with languages which is interesting.

"Let's go and find this girl." I give them the coordinates and they all cheer, hop in the transportation, and off they go.

I follow them, leaving this building and heading to Eastleigh.

Aftermath 2

I find out that it is over and the mystery is solved. I head to the Caribbean for a lovely sun and water time with no disturbance at all. It will be great getting there. The ghost made a gate in the café. I look as Charlette gestures to me. I end up in the Caribbean and I watch the others go to their destinations.

Washington and Rose are already walking around Ortez in the South of France on a cold night. Next, it is the leaning Tower of Pisa where Tillie is. I see a big street and a bullring shopping centre where Richard is. I turn to walk in. Finally, it was a shopping centre in Southampton where Paige runs through.

The ghost says to me, "Hannah, you are a nice person. Please stay safe and do not get hurt. Be careful, and good luck to you. Your power is strong as a team." Before it leaves, it hands me a bag. Inside, there are tools I need. I grab the bag and I will look after it with my life. Also taking in those words, they hit my heart.

I sit on the beach in the Caribbean and then find a sunbed. I lay in the sun eyeing the bag from time to time. I get curious so I open the bag. It is a book and I open it. The page shows me the Care Home. I turn the page and it shows France and I see Washington and Rose, then Tillie in Italy, and the last two in their places. It is cool to see. There is also something written.

Dear Hannah

I hope you look after your friends and keep them out of danger.

P.S. I hope you enjoy the beach and the sun.

From Charlette and the team at the Care Home.

It makes me smile. I close the book and put it back in the bag. While doing so, I see the stick is here with me. So, I put it in the bag too. I won't need it till later. I zip the bag and lie in the sun, enjoying the moment.

Aftermath 3

All the villains that go to prison, go through security. They enter the cells and the doors close. They look out as the guards walk up and down in separate places. Lauren is on the top left, Harley is in the middle, Lily is on the right of the top floor and Janet is in the middle on the right.

They are keeping us apart and we want to hurt these people. Lights go out and all go to sleep. A guard walks past me with headphones in. I peer out and he goes to another one on the same floor as me. The girl yells and the bars shift out of the wall. He taps with the baton and it goes quiet. Night falls in the prison.

I whisper, "We will get you, heroes of the Care Home, and bring hell." I lay in the bed provided and close my eyes, drifting into a deep sleep.

The End, or is it?

Printed in Great Britain
by Amazon

42432145R00086